"Not so fast."

A hand suddenly closed around Celina's arm, and she was brought to an abrupt halt.

"This may not be a marriage for all the traditional reasons," Reid told her, "but you have traditional-minded neighbors."

In the next instant, Celina found herself being swept up into her new husband's arms and carried toward the front porch. His after-shave filled her senses. In spite of the layers of clothing between them, she felt the heat of his body. Her heart began to pound even more rapidly.

When they reached the door, Reid set her on her feet just long enough to unlock it. Then, lifting her again, he carried his bride over the threshold.

Celina's breath threatened to lock in her lungs as she waited for Reid to continue with her up the stairs to the bedroom they would share....

Dear Reader,

June . . . a month of courtship and romance, white lace and wedding vows. And at Silhouette Romance we're celebrating those June brides and grooms with some very special tales of love and marriage. Best of all—YOU'RE INVITED!

As every bride knows, you can't march down the aisle without the essentials, starting with *Something Old*—a fun-filled look at love with an older man—from Toni Collins. Gabriella Thorne falls for her boss, Adrian Lacross—a handsome and oh-so-charming . . . vampire. Can the love of a good woman change Adrian's fly-by-night romantic ways?

Something New was in store for prim-and-proper Eve Winthrop the day the new high school principal came to town. Carla Cassidy brings us the *irresistible* Brice Maxwell, who shakes up a sleepy Oklahoma town and dares Eve to take a walk on the wild side.

Linda Varner brings us *Something Borrowed* from the magical land of Oz! A tornado whisked Brooke Brady into Patrick Sawyer's life. Is handsome Patrick really a heartless Tin Man—or Brooke's very own heart's desire?

Something Blue is an unexpected little package from the stork for newly divorced Teddy Falco and Quinn Barnett. Jayne Addison's heartwarming style lends special magic to this story of a couple reunited by the miracle of their new baby.

Elizabeth August gives the final touch to our wedding bouquet with *Lucky Penny*. Celina Warley and Reid Prescott weren't looking for a marriage with love, but with luck, would love find them?

Our FABULOUS FATHERS series continues with an unforgettable hero and dad—Judd Tanner, in *One Man's Vow* by Diana Whitney. Judd is a devoted father who will go the limit to protect his four children—even if it means missing out on the love of one very special woman.

In the months to come look for books by more of your favorite authors—Annette Broadrick, Diana Palmer, Lucy Gordon, Suzanne Carey and many more.

Until then, happy reading!

Anne Canadeo
Senior Editor

LUCKY PENNY
Elizabeth August

Silhouette
ROMANCE™
Published by Silhouette Books New York
America's Publisher of Contemporary Romance

To David and Teresa—
Happy first anniversary and may each succeeding
year be even better than the one before.

SILHOUETTE BOOKS
300 East 42nd St., New York, N.Y. 10017

LUCKY PENNY

Copyright © 1993 by Elizabeth August

ISBN: 0-373-08945-7

First Silhouette Books printing June 1993

Printed in the U.S.A.

ELIZABETH AUGUST

has been married for twenty-five years. "If I had to choose the one aspect of our marriage that has been the most important to me, it would be our friendship. His support and encouragement have helped me through some very difficult times, and I like to think I've given him the support he's needed. Like good friends, we know each other's strengths and admire them. He's an optimist and I'm a pessimist. He's methodical and patient in his approach to life while I generally jump in without looking. The end result is that we balance each other fairly well.

"He doesn't always say the right thing at the right time, but the fact that I know he wants to is what's important. I plan to stick around for another twenty-five years."

Reid Prescott on marriage:

I'd never planned on walking down the aisle. Love and marriage is fine for other people but I have no interest in playing games of the heart. However, *this* marriage has nothing to do with love. It's simply a practical solution to both mine and Celina's problems. And, unlike those romantics who enter marriage with notions of joyful togetherness, she and I have no illusions and, therefore, no chance of being hurt.

Celina Warley on marriage:

Marriage to Reid Prescott is a means to an end. He needs a wife to get what he wants. I want a child. Having a husband will make my pregnancy more socially acceptable. And, I have to admit, I am physically attracted to Reid. As long as I don't do something foolish, such as fall in love with him and begin to hope our marriage will last, this arrangement should work out just fine.

Prologue

Celina Warley marveled at how deeply the weed she was trying to extract from her front garden was rooted. All the others had been coming out easily. She shoved her trowel deep into the dirt beside the tenacious root to loosen the soil. Her next pull was successful and the weed came out, root and all. A clump of dirt came along with it. Crumbling the clump in her hand, she found a small round object embedded within. Rubbing it clean enough to discover what it was, she saw it was a penny.

"A buried treasure," she murmured jestingly to herself and shoved it into her pocket.

Chapter One

Dr. Reid Prescott was furious. He'd had his fill of faith healers. Discovering there was one in this small conservative Massachusetts town had been a surprise. Although her presence had nagged at the back of his mind, he'd managed to avoid her—until now. As he parked in front of Celina Warley's home on this hot August afternoon, he saw her. She was on her hands and knees weeding the flower garden that bordered her front porch, her back toward him. He saw a mass of thick auburn hair loosely braided into a single thick plait from which several strands were escaping to hang in wet tendrils along her neck. His gaze traveled to her sweat-dampened T-shirt clinging to her firm straight back, which she was now stretching by sitting back on her heels and moving her shoulders. Next came shapely hips encased in a pair of faded jean shorts and finally the bottoms of a pair of old worn sneakers.

He knew when she stood and turned around he'd see a reasonably pleasant-featured face and a figure that would best be described as hourglass, with its full bust, narrow waist and rounded hips. He remembered the first time he'd seen her walking down the street. Scowling, he recalled the spark of attraction he'd felt.

"That's Celina Warley," Dr. Theodore James had told him, noticing the direction of Reid's gaze. "She's our town librarian and healer."

Dr. James had laughed lightly at this last pronouncement, but Reid had immediately put Celina Warley on his list of people he would stay away from. During the time he'd been in Smytheshire, he'd learned that Dr. James and Celina had a friendly relationship, but Reid Prescott had no intention of even giving the lady the time of day. He did, however, intend to give her a piece of his mind.

Passing through the gate of the white picket fence that bordered the yard of the large, old-fashioned two-story frame house, he approached her. When she didn't turn around, he came to a halt about five feet behind her. His anger had been building with each step. Now standing with his feet slightly straddled and his hands on his hips, he glared down at her back. "It's against the law to practice medicine without a license," he growled.

His ire grew as she continued to work in her garden as if he wasn't even there. "You could at least have the common courtesy to face me," he seethed, attempting to keep his voice below a bellow, but just barely succeeding.

"She can't hear you." Reid looked to his right to see a blond-haired boy in his teens coming around the corner of the house. He recognized the youth as Josh Sayer. The boy was carrying a hoe and had obviously been working in another garden somewhere on the side of house. "She's deaf. But she can read lips real good," Josh continued, watching Reid with a worried expression on his face.

"She's deaf?" Reid repeated. He'd heard a lot about Celina during the few months he'd been here, but no one had ever mentioned she was deaf.

Josh nodded. "Happened in the plane crash that killed her parents."

Reid drew a harsh breath as a wave of sympathy for the woman swept over him. Then the sympathy vanished. She still had no right to place other people's lives in danger. Taking a step closer, he tapped her on the shoulder.

Celina jerked upright as a startling current of power shot through her. Certain Josh had injured himself, panic filled her. She turned her head expecting to see a hand covered with blood. Instead the hand in front of her face looked perfectly healthy. Not only that, it wasn't Josh's youthful work-callused hand. This hand was larger, less callused and the fingers squarer. Her gaze traveled up the arm to which the hand was attached, and she found herself looking into the angry face of Dr. Reid Prescott.

She'd never met him, but she knew who he was. Everyone in their small community knew everyone else. A newcomer was immediately the source of gossip and speculation. A new doctor was of even more interest. His bags had hardly been unpacked before nearly all the locals knew his name and the fact that he'd grown up mostly in New York City and done his internship at a major hospital there. But ever since he'd arrived in town, she'd had the distinct feeling that he'd gone out of his way to avoid her. She wasn't sure why. However, he made her nervous and so she hadn't minded keeping a distance between them. Now here he was glowering down at her as if she'd committed some heinous crime.

Reid took a step back as Celina rose to her feet and turned to face him. He'd seen the anxiousness on her face when she'd glanced over her shoulder. She probably knows she placed Debra Ramsey in danger, he thought, the coldness in his eyes increasing.

Celina's shoulders squared. Obviously Reid Prescott was angry with her, but she had no idea why. She certainly hadn't done anything that should offend him

Studying her, Reid wondered if she knew sign language. Josh had said she read lips. But Reid wanted to be sure she understood just how serious an offense she'd committed. Glad he'd learned signing to communicate with the deaf patients who had been brought into the emergency room of the hospital where he'd interned, his hands began to move, forming the words he was speaking. "You should have sent Debra Ramsey to me immediately. Both her and her unborn child are at high risk. I should have been treating them from the beginning of her pregnancy."

Not only could Celina see the anger on his face, she could even see it in his hands; their sharp movements giving evidence of how enraged he was. Her shoulders squared even more with self-righteous indignation. "This morning was the first time she's ever come to see me. I told her she had to go see Dr. James or you immediately."

Reid raised a skeptical eyebrow. Not only did he not believe this declaration, the clearness with which she had spoken made him question her claim of deafness. "For someone who can't hear, you speak very well," he observed, wondering what kind of game this woman was playing.

Celina watched his lips moving. She couldn't hear his voice, but she could see the accusation in his eyes. "I was fifteen when the accident happened," she said, confused by his finding her ability to speak offensive and growing irritated with his hostile manner. "I already knew how to pronounce words properly, and Doc worked hard with me to make sure I didn't forget."

Reid was forced to admit that would explain her speaking skill. His jaw tensed as he continued to study the woman in front of him. The sun glinting on her auburn hair brought out its reddish highlights. And he didn't think he'd ever seen eyes so intensely brown. He found himself thinking she looked rather cute. But dangerous, he added, noting the developing anger on her face. The streak of dirt smeared across her cheek was the final touch that caused him to think of a street urchin preparing for a fight. Then he scowled at himself. She was dangerous, but not to him. The people who thought she was a healer were the ones to whom she posed a danger.

"You might as well know right now, Miss Warley, that I don't believe in healers like you. I've seen the damage you can do. I had a child die in my arms because his parents took him to a healer, instead of seeking proper medical help. I won't let that happen again." Reid had been speaking and signing at the same time. As he finished, he banged his fist hard into his hand to give emphasis to his words.

"Celina would never do that," Josh said.

Celina had been so aware of Reid Prescott she'd forgotten about the boy's presence. Now she saw Reid's attention jerk to his right. Glancing that way also, she saw Josh moving toward her, an expression of protectiveness on his face.

Reid watched the boy approach the woman. *The people in this town do stick together,* he thought, *even if it isn't always for their own good.* "I hope you're right," he said curtly, as the image of the dying child remained vivid in his mind. Turning abruptly, he strode back to his car and left.

Celina felt a tap on her shoulder. It caused her to jump slightly. Her attention had turned back to Reid Prescott and she'd again forgotten Josh's presence. Stunned that the man could so fully claim her mind, she gave herself a shake.

"Are you all right?" Josh asked.

Celina smiled to alleviate the worry on his face. "I'm fine. I've never let bullies bother me."

Josh frowned, confusion mingling with the concern on his face. Using the signing Celina had taught him, he said, "I've never seen Dr. Prescott fly off the handle like that before. I've always thought he was a nice person, quiet...calm."

Celina was still smarting from the accusations Reid Prescott had thrown at her. But she was forced to recall the pain she'd seen in his eyes when he'd mentioned the dying child. "He's just concerned about his patients," she said, surprised to find herself coming to his defense. *I'm doing it because it's the fair thing to do,* she reasoned, but couldn't stop herself from adding aloud, "But he should get his facts straight before he indicts a person."

"Don't let him upset you," Josh said solicitously, his hands moving with firm command.

Celina smiled. Emily Sayer had raised her son well, she thought. And as an unwed mother disowned by her family, Emily had done it primarily on her own. "Let's get these gardens weeded," she said, her tone indicating that she intended to put the incident with Dr. Prescott out of her mind.

Josh nodded and headed back around the house.

As she turned back to her garden, a notion that had been plaguing Celina for the past several months again played through her mind. Her jaw formed a resolute line. She set the trowel aside and pulled off her gloves.

"I'll be back in a few minutes," she called out to Josh as she headed into the house for her car keys.

A short while later she parked in front of Doctor James's office. She knew he would have already left for the day but she hoped Glenda Jones, his nurse-receptionist, would still be there. Luck was with her. Glenda was there catching up on paperwork and Celina was able to make an appointment to see Doc the next morning.

Reid Prescott was still angry when he reached Theodore James's house. For more than forty years Theodore had been the only doctor in Smytheshire. He ran an old-fashioned family practice, the kind that saw patients through from birth to death. Now that he was nearing seventy, he was looking for someone to take over, and Reid was there on a trial basis to see if he and the job were suited to each other.

Doc, which was what most of the residents of the town called Theodore James, had invited Reid to lodge with him. Reid hadn't wanted to impose but the older man had been insistent. "Since my wife died, this old house seems downright empty. I'd like the company," Doc had said. So, Reid had accepted the invitation.

The house was certainly large enough for the two of them, Reid had to admit as he mounted the steps to the wide front porch of the large, two-story frame house, so similar to the majority of homes in this town.

"Glenda told me you went to see Celina," Doc said in a questioning tone as Reid reached the porch.

Reid stood looking at the long, lanky white-haired man seated in the big wooden chair with his feet propped up on the porch railing. "Yes, I did."

"Been thinking I should talk to you about Celina," Doc said, continuing to study the younger man. "Seems like you developed an instant dislike for her. Don't understand that. She's a pleasant girl."

Reid read the concern in the older man's eyes. He knew Doc took his obligation of choosing a new doctor for Smytheshire very seriously. Reid would find the cost of beginning a new practice prohibitive if Doc didn't think he was the man for the job. He'd have to purchase all his own equipment and rent office space at the going rate. Whereas, if Doc gave him the nod of approval, he would be offered the same deal Doc had.

Doc's offices were located next door to his home in a building owned by the Smythes. Their patriarch, Angus Smythe, had founded Smytheshire and been the town's leading benefactor. Wanting to assure the townsfolk of proper medical care, Angus had built and equipped the small medical facility. And, his family continued to see that its equipment was kept up to date. Reid had been surprised to find such an elaborate setup for a one-man practice. Doc's offices were better stocked than some small clinics Reid had seen. Reid had also discovered that the Smythes had paid to have Glenda Jones and Karen Zeberly, the two nurses who worked for Doc, trained in the use of the equipment. And there was a standing arrangement that the Smythes would pay to have that same training provided for any new nurses whenever there was a change of staff. For all of this—the office and the equipment—Doc paid one dollar a year.

But Reid Prescott wasn't willing to sell his values for any price. His feet spread slightly into a combative stance. "I don't approve of healers," he said. "I've seen the damage they can do."

Doc breathed a heavy sigh. "Seems my little jest backfired."

"Jest?" Reid questioned sharply.

"Have a seat," Doc said, indicating the porch chair beside his with a wave of his arm. "We need to have a little talk. We'll consider this a consultation, so that what I tell you is confidential and can go no further."

"You might consider Miss Warley's reputation as a healer a joke," Reid said grimly as he seated himself. "But others in this town don't, and that could prove dangerous to them if they seek her help, instead of coming to you or me."

"Celina wouldn't let that happen," Doc replied firmly.

Reid had grown to respect Doc. But now he wondered if the old man wasn't letting a cute young face influence him. "How can you be so sure?"

"I know Celina," Doc replied with conviction, then added, "Fact is, I'm sort of responsible for her reputation as a healer."

Reid studied the older man. He'd been working with Theodore James now for months, and he knew this man to be an excellent doctor and not one who would deal in quack methods. "You're responsible?" he asked sharply.

Leaning farther back in his chair, Doc stared out at his front lawn and the street beyond. A soft smile played across his face. "I delivered that girl." The smile vanished. "And I doctored her after the plane crash that killed her parents. Happened just outside town. Her dad was a pilot. He had his own plane and had built a small landing strip on his farm. He earned a little extra money ferrying people around once in a while but mostly his flying was a hobby. The day of the crash, he was flying his family up to Canada to visit his brother. The experts say it was some sort of wind rip that caused the accident. Anyway, young Kenneth and his wife were killed. It was a miracle Celina survived. She was in a coma by the time we got her to the hospital. But she was a fighter." Doc's jaw tensed. "I was there when she awoke. I can still recall the look of terror in her eyes as if she expected to see the plane coming down."

Reid felt a surge of sympathy for Celina. He hadn't known much about her until now. He'd just assumed she was a kook or a shyster. The truth was, he admitted, he'd gone out of his way *not* to learn anything about her.

Doc breathed a heavy sigh. "Then we discovered that the trauma she'd experienced to the head had left her deaf. It didn't seem fair. For a while she was angry. But her family, both sides—the Tuppers and the Warleys—rallied around her. The whole town did. We're a small community here. A close-knit one. People here take care of their own. That's one of the reasons I like Smytheshire so much. Anyway, Helen Ashbey knew sign language. Her grandmother had been deaf from birth and Helen had learned it years ago. She taught Celina and held classes for anyone else in town who wanted to learn. With Helen there to interpret, the teachers at the school gave Celina private tutoring.''

''She was lucky to have all of you in her corner,'' Reid said, thinking not for the first time that this was the kind of town he'd always wanted to settle down in.

''True,'' Doc said. ''Still, there was a sadness about her... Maybe 'sadness' isn't the right word. An incompleteness. It was as if she was trying to find where she fitted in. Not that her family didn't shower her with love. They did. But there was this sort of lost look in her eyes I'd see every once in a while. And she began to withdraw into herself.''

Reid recalled the Celina Warley he'd faced a few minutes earlier. ''She sure didn't have any 'lost' look in her eyes when I faced her a little while ago,'' he said. ''And she sure didn't look like she'd withdrawn from the world.''

Doc grinned. ''Nope. Celina's found her place.'' His expression became thoughtful. ''It all started with Daniel Kolby. He was a cute baby but was always crying up a storm. I checked him over a hundred times and everything seemed all right. But his mother was slowly becoming a wreck from lack of sleep and it got so no one wanted to baby-sit the child to give her a break. Then, I think it was Edna Warley, Celina's grandmother, who thought of Celina—the girl couldn't hear the baby's howling, so she could tend to him without getting a headache. Not that Celina neglected the baby when she was with him. She'd hold him and talk to him. In fact, taking care of him sort of brought her out of herself.

"Guess she'd been taking care of him for about two days when she came to see me. She said she'd noticed that a spot on his back felt downright hot to her, but his mother hadn't felt any unusual heat. I could tell Celina was worried that the trauma she'd suffered in the accident was having another damaging effect on her. She asked me if I'd go check on the baby. Didn't seem reasonable to me that one spot on the baby's body would feel scorching hot and the rest of him wouldn't, but I figured I'd humor her. I took her back over to the Kolby house and we checked on the baby together. I couldn't feel anything, but I did notice that Daniel let out a howl when I prodded him where Celina said she felt the heat.

"Up till then, I'd thought the boy was just colicky. His mother was the overly fussy type, and that makes for a nervous child sometimes. Anyway, I decided that just to be safe I'd have his parents take him into Boston and have some tests run. Turned out he had a cyst on one of his kidneys. It was enlarging and causing pain. The doctors there operated and were able to remove it without causing any damage to the kidney. The baby was a real joy after that—a little spoiled, but a good kid. Lucky for him Celina caught the trouble before it could do any real damage."

Doc paused and shook his head at this memory. "Anyway, that little incident got me curious. Celina was living with her dad's parents at the time. I went by to see her. While I was there, I asked her to touch her grandmother's ankles. Edna was beginning to develop arthritis pretty bad in her right ankle and some in her left. Celina said the right one felt hotter than the left. Then Edna told me that she liked to have Celina massage her ankles because the girl's touch was so soothing.''

Doc frowned introspectively. "I was watching Celina. She seemed so vibrant when she was touching her grandmother. 'Seems she might have a healer's touch,' I said. 'Don't know about her being able to heal these old bones,' Edna said, 'but she sure can make them feel better.' I explained real quick that I didn't think Celina could cure anyone but that she did seem to have a knack for being able to spot where they might be having some trouble.''

Doc grimaced. "'Course you know how rumors go. Before long people were whispering that the girl was a healer. A few people started showing up at Edna's door for help. That was when Celina and I had a long talk. She'd always been a sensible girl. We made an agreement. If anyone came to her, she was to let me know. And if she touched them and felt any unusual warmth she was to let me know that, too. Through the years we've developed a real good system. Sometimes when I'm not sure a patient is really sick or I can't find any reason for the pain they're having, I'll ask her to come in and touch them. If she feels something, then I know I'd better run my tests again.''

Reid's eyebrows rose skeptically. "Are you telling me that you honestly believe she can detect a medical problem by simply touching a person?" he asked, wondering if he'd misjudged Doc. Maybe the man wasn't as rational as he'd thought.

"Yes," Doc replied with conviction.

Reid studied the elderly man narrowly. "You really believe that," he said, his voice suggesting he was worried that Doc might be suffering from a touch of senility.

Theodore James met the younger man's gaze levelly. "You've told me you like Smytheshire and want to stay. I've watched you. You're good with your patients. You're a bit cool, but you treat them with respect and kindness. And, you're a good doctor." He lowered his voice slightly. "I'm going to tell you something about this town, as one doctor to another. That makes what I say confidential."

The hint of conspiracy in Doc's manner caused Reid's concern for Doc to increase. "Whatever you tell me won't go any farther," he said, humoring the older man.

"I'd been practicing medicine here for about six years when old Angus Smythe invited me to his house for dinner one night," Doc said. "He was in his eighties then. During the meal he asked me about my impression of the town and its people. I said the town seemed typical of what I thought a small town would be like and that the people were mostly a pleasant lot. I had the feeling he wanted me to say more, but there wasn't anything more to say. After the meal we went into his study. Angus said he wanted to have a private consultation with me—that what he was going to tell me I should consider a doctor-patient confidence. I told him, 'Of course.' I figured he was going to tell me he thought he had cancer or some other life-threatening disease. Instead, he started telling me about his lineage."

Doc paused to shake his head. "Most people can't trace their ancestry back more than three or four generations. Angus Smythe claimed he could trace his back to pre-Christian times. He claimed he was descended from a family from which members of the druid priesthood had been chosen. Then he told me that a large percentage of the population of this town was from families with a similar lineage. It seems that his ancestors had kept track of these other families, and he'd started this town as a means of gathering them together again."

A chill ran along Reid's spine. He studied Doc dubiously. "Are you telling me that while on the surface this looks like a normal, sane, quiet farming community, beneath that facade are a bunch of practicing pagans?"

Doc held up his hands. "No. No. The people here are mostly Congregationalists or Presbyterians. There's a few Catholics and a couple of atheists. But no practicing druids. In fact, according to Angus and from my own knowledge, very, very few even know of their supposed ancestry. And those that do aren't passing the information on. It's supposed to be a secret."

"But Angus told you," Reid pointed out, still having some trouble digesting this information and beginning to worry more seriously about the possibility of Doc's mind not being totally sound.

Doc smiled patronizingly. "I know what I'm telling you seems a bit farfetched," he said. "But it's what Angus told me. He said he gathered the descendants of those families here with the hope that the mystical powers his ancestors supposedly possessed would reemerge. He'd been patiently waiting, he told me, but other than a few isolated instances of ESP, to his knowledge nothing spectacular had happened. He wanted me to keep an eye out for anything unusual and report it to him."

"And *did* you report to him?" Reid asked, needing to know just how far Doc had been drawn into this craziness.

Doc grinned at the concern in Reid's eyes. "You don't have to worry about trucking me off to the state asylum," he said with a chuckle. "I humored the old man. I told him I'd keep an eye out for anything unusual. But I never passed anything on. I have to admit, there were a few incidents that surprised me, but then life is full of oddities. Then Celina's 'ability' surfaced. She got me to seriously thinking about what Angus had said. It occurred to me that the hardest part of our job as physicians is diagnosing the ailment. We have to know what we're dealing with before we even have a chance of curing it. Following that line of reasoning, it seemed to me that the more successful ancient healers were probably terrific diagnosticians. So if what Angus told me was actually true, then Celina's ancestors were probably healers in a pre-Christian society, and she inherited her unique ability from them. It was most likely lying dormant inside of her and when she lost her hearing, it emerged as a sixth sense to compensate for the loss of one of her original five."

That he found a certain amount of logic in what Doc was saying shook Reid. "I still don't like the idea of people going to Celina Warley when they need real medical assistance," he said stiffly.

"But she always sends them to us, and even if she doesn't detect anything wrong, she tells me that they've been to see her," Doc countered.

Still frowning disapprovingly, Reid directed his gaze to the street in front of him. On the other side, a little way up, was the fire station. Toward town was the building that housed the police station and city offices. It all looked so normal, so peaceful. And it was. He'd expected Doc's revelations to make him feel uneasy now about this town and its people, but he didn't. Because, this druid business was silliness, he scoffed mentally. Even if Angus Smythe was right about his ancestry and that of a large portion of the population here, they were living in the modern world now. What was magic in pre-Christian times was merely superstition today and could be easily explained away.

"Speaking of Celina sending people to see us," Doc said, interrupting Reid's thoughts, "she came by about midmorning and told me that Debra Ramsey needed to see one of us. I noticed you had a break in your schedule, so I had Karen put her on your list."

Reid's expression grew black. "She's the reason I went to see Miss Warley. Mrs. Ramsey is into her fourth month of a very threatening pregnancy. She should have been coming to see us from the very first instead of seeking help from Miss Warley."

"I can't believe Celina has been trying to treat her," Doc said, clearly shaken by the implication in Reid's words that Celina had been ministering to the pregnant woman.

"Miss Warley did claim that today was the first time Debra Ramsey had come to see her," Reid admitted.

Doc looked relieved. "I told you Celina is level-headed." Then he frowned. "Did she happen to mention why Debra went to see her instead of coming directly to us?''

"I didn't ask. I just assumed it was common practice for Debra Ramsey to go to her," Reid replied, realizing he'd done a great deal of accusing and very little questioning.

Doc shook his head. "No, it's not. There's something going on with Debra Ramsey that she won't talk about," he continued, worry etched into his features. "I've been taking care of her since the day she was born. If she has the flu, a cut, a broken bone, anything like that, she comes to me. But when I suggested she was old enough to begin having yearly pap smears, she balked. And when she comes in for a physical, she refuses to allow me to do an internal exam. Of course some women are overly modest. But I find it hard to think of her as being that way."

Reid recalled his examination of the twenty-five-year-old woman. "She was very nervous and tense," he said. "Both Glenda and I tried to put her at ease but she acted frightened the entire time. I chalked it up to concern about losing her baby."

"And is that a real possibility?" Doc asked.

"Yes," Reid confirmed. "She's developed diabetes with this pregnancy. She's going to have to take very good care of herself."

Chapter Two

Reid frowned. He'd been restless all evening. After dinner, he'd given in to the need for some physical exertion and gone out for a walk, but he couldn't believe where his legs had carried him. Just ahead of him was Celina Warley's house.

Well, she did deserve an apology, he told himself. And he was worried about Debra Ramsey. If Celina knew something that would explain the woman's fright, he wanted to know what it was.

Celina was sitting in a rocking chair on her front porch knitting. Instead of the peacefulness she usually experienced on one of these lovely summer nights, the sense of isolation that had been tormenting her all day prevailed. She considered her options. She could walk over to her Grandma and Grandpa Tupper's home. Or she could stroll over to see Aunt Adelle. Or she could drive out to Grandma and Grandpa Warley's farm. But if she went to visit any of them, she might tell them what she was planning and they were sure to try to dissuade her. Her jaw firmed. And that would probably lead to an argument because she was determined not to be dissuaded.

A movement caught her eye. Looking up from her knitting, she saw Reid Prescott coming through her gate. Her body tensed. She shoved her knitting into the canvas bag beside her chair and rose. "Was there some accusation you forgot to fling at me?" she asked dryly as he mounted the steps to the porch.

"I've come to apologize," he signed.

Following his motions, Celina found herself fascinated by the strength and form of his hands. She recalled the surge of power she'd felt when he'd tapped her on the shoulder earlier that afternoon, and a heat stirred within her. *Reid Prescott thinks I'm a menace to society,* she reminded herself. The warmth turned to a chill as she faced him squarely.

"Doc explained the arrangement he has with you," Reid continued, this time speaking as he signed. "I still don't approve of the idea of people coming to you. But it seems that this isn't your choice, and he swears you don't try to cure them."

Seeing the skepticism in his eyes, her back straightened even more. "No, I do not try to cure them. I know my limitations, Dr. Prescott," she assured him.

"That's very wise of you," he replied.

Because she couldn't hear the nuances in their voices, Celina had learned to study people, both their faces and their body language. She saw his hesitation and the slight shift of his shoulders, as if he was uneasy. *He doesn't want to be here,* she decided and felt the sting of insult. *Well, I don't want his company either.* "You've made your apology and I've accepted it," she said. "Good evening, Doctor." It was getting dark now. With the intent of going inside, she turned away from him and started to pick up the canvas sack holding her knitting.

"I have something else I need to talk to you about," Reid said to her back. When she didn't respond, he groaned mentally. Reaching out, he tapped her on the shoulder.

Celina jerked around as once again a startling current of energy raced through her.

"There is something else I need to talk to you about," Reid repeated.

Celina noted the determined set of his jaw. Clearly he expected her to cause him some trouble. Well, he was the one who had declared them enemies, she reminded herself. "What is it?" she asked levelly.

Catching a glimpse of Julia and Paul Johnson strolling down the street, he motioned toward the door. "Could we step inside?" he requested. "I'd like this to be a private conversation."

Following his line of vision, Celina, too, saw the Johnsons. In the dimming light she saw Julia sign a good-evening and signed one back.

As Celina motioned for him to precede her into the house, Reid congratulated himself for not assuming that their conversation would be private simply because it could be conducted in silence. Inside, he was struck by the cozy comfortable atmosphere of her home. Celina Warley, however, was not looking at him with a welcoming smile.

She stopped just a few feet inside the house. Normally she would have invited guests into the living room and offered them something cold to drink, but Reid Prescott wasn't a guest. He was only here because he wanted something from her. "What do you want to talk to me about?" she asked.

"It's about Debra Ramsey," Reid signed. "Doc seems to think there's a reason she came to see you, instead of coming to us first."

Celina frowned. She'd counseled Debra to tell the doctors everything. Obviously the woman hadn't taken her advice. If this had been Doc asking, Celina admitted, she would not have hesitated to tell him what she knew. But with Reid Prescott, she found herself holding back. "What do you think?" she asked.

Celina Warley was good at playing innocent, Reid thought. But he was sure she knew something she wasn't telling him. Well, he hadn't exactly behaved like someone who deserved her trust, he admitted. "Debra was nervous and scared," he said slowly, signing as he spoke. "I've seen women act like that when they're afraid they're pregnant and don't want to be. But that isn't the case with Debra. She wants her baby." His gaze narrowed on Celina. "For her sake and the sake of the baby, I need to know if there is something about this pregnancy she isn't telling me."

Celina saw the concern in his eyes. It was the same look she'd seen in Doc's eyes when he was worried about a patient. And if Reid Prescott took over for Doc, she was going to have to try to work with him— at least report to him if anyone came to see her. She doubted, though, he'd ever ask her for her help.

"Debra came to see me because she knew there was something wrong with her pregnancy, but she was afraid to go to you or Doc," she said. "When she was fifteen, she had an affair with a boy from Greenfield. Actually, a man. He was twenty-three at the time and married. But she didn't know about his marriage until it was too late. She wasn't even supposed to be dating. Her parents thought she was out with a girlfriend when she went out with him. She doesn't make any excuses. She admits she behaved foolishly. Anyway, she got pregnant. The man was furious. He gave her an envelope with money inside for expenses and told her never to contact him again. He said he'd claim she lied to him about her age, seduced him and then asked for money for her services.''

Celina paused to scowl at the mean-heartedness of some people, then went on. ''Debra was crushed and scared. She was too ashamed to tell her parents. She got more and more anxious and panicky, trying to decide what to do. Her grandmother on her mother's side was a widow living alone on a small farm in New Hampshire. She and Debra had always been especially close and Debra trusted her discretion. She talked her parents into letting her go visit the elderly woman for the summer. She became ill and miscarried during her third month. The grandmother helped her keep the whole thing a secret.''

Celina again paused for a moment, then continued, ''Debra decided that before she married Neil, she should tell him everything. But when she got as far as confessing to the affair, she could see he was extremely upset. She got scared and didn't tell him about the pregnancy. She was afraid of losing him.'' Celina regarded Reid narrowly. ''The reason she was so nervous around you is that she's afraid if you discovered the truth, you'd tell Neil.''

Reid scowled impatiently. ''Doesn't she know about doctor-patient confidentiality?''

"She knows but she's still worried," Celina replied, signing with sharp gestures to give emphasis to her words. "If she tells you, she's afraid it'll have to go in her records and your nurses will see it."

"Our nurses are trustworthy," Reid returned, signing with gestures just as sharp.

Celina frowned impatiently. "The woman is scared for her marriage."

Reid drew a terse breath. Sympathetic concern replaced the impatience on his face. "I do understand her position," he admitted, signing in more fluid motions. "I've met Neil Ramsey. He's not a tolerant man. He lives by a rigid code of conduct, and from what I've seen and heard, he expects his wife to live by it too. I suspect Debra could be right. The knowledge of her affair might have strained his tolerance as far as it'll go." He paused for a moment, then added, "I'll find a way to assure her that her secret is safe with me."

Celina read the earnestness on his face and knew that Debra could trust him. "Thanks," she said.

Reid meant to thank her for her cooperation, say goodbye and leave. Instead, he found himself drawn into the depths of a pair of hickory-brown eyes. Startled by the heat that flared within him, he shifted his gaze. It fell on her lips. They looked soft and invitingly kissable. *Celina Warley is not someone you want to get involved with,* he admonished himself. *She's the kind of woman who would want a commitment.* Finding these unexpected jolts of attraction toward this woman difficult to cope with, he frowned down at his watch. "I'd better be going," he said as if he had an urgent appointment.

Celina drew a shaky breath. She'd never looked into a pair of eyes so intensely blue. For one brief moment, a fire had ignited within her. Now it was nothing but cold ashes as she watched him. He was speaking, but he was looking down and she couldn't read his lips. There was a brusqueness in his manner, however, that told her he was anxious to be on his way.

Glancing up, Reid saw Celina watching him. Again he mentally kicked himself. He'd forgotten she wouldn't know what he was saying if he wasn't looking at her. "I have to be going," he repeated. He tapped his watch as if he had an urgent appointment. Then after signing, "Thank you for your cooperation," he strode outside.

As he passed through her gate, he scowled at himself. His reactions to Celina Warley still had him feeling shaken. Clearly he'd been without female companionship far too long.

Watching him from her doorway, Celina frowned at his departing back. Once his business had been completed, he'd nearly raced out of her place. Obviously she and Dr. Prescott were not going to be friends. Considering the brevity of their conversations, she could barely classify them as acquaintances!

Going back outside, she sat down in the rocking chair and looked up at the night sky. The moon was a lovely crescent. Drawing in a deep breath of the warm summer air, she closed her eyes. Suddenly a pair of startling blue eyes filled her inner vision. Her own eyes popped open. *I'm so lonely, I'm even thinking about Reid Prescott,* she mused dryly. Well, she had a solution to her loneliness, and tomorrow she would begin working on it.

* * *

Celina sat in one of Doc's examining rooms. Beneath the wraparound gown Glenda had given her to change into, she was wearing nothing so that Doc could do a thorough exam. Nervously she watched the door. The thought of the exam didn't bother her. It was Doc's reaction to the request she was going to make that made her uneasy. The door opened and she gasped.

Without looking into the room, Reid lifted the file out of the holder on the examining room door. "Dr. James is having to take longer with another patient than he anticipated. Glenda thought you wouldn't mind if I—" He stopped in midsentence. He hadn't read the name on the file when he retrieved it. Now, as he turned toward the examining table, he found himself staring into the shocked face of Celina Warley.

Because Reid had been speaking swiftly and not looking directly at her as he entered, Celina hadn't been able to discern what he'd been saying. Assuming he'd simply come into the wrong examining room, she said pointedly, "I have an appointment to see Doc."

"He's being detained," Reid replied, then turned his attention to her file. He didn't like admitting it, but he was as nervous as if this was his first time ever to examine a patient. Actually, he hadn't been this nervous the first time, he amended. Setting aside the folder, he looked at her. "Glenda said you're here for a physical," he signed as he spoke. "Have you been having any pains or symptoms I should know about?"

The thought of Reid Prescott performing the exam filled her with panic. *He's a doctor*, she told herself. But all she could think about was how those large strong hands of his would feel when they touched her.

And this thought was causing a heated excitement to race through her. "I'm perfectly healthy," she assured him, fighting the urge to grab her clothes and run.

Turning his back toward her, Reid feigned an intense interest in her file. He'd examined hundreds of women, he reminded himself curtly. Many had been prettier than Celina Warley, and he'd had no trouble maintaining an indifferent, purely academic attitude toward them. But the thought of what she looked like beneath that gown was causing a heat within him that was totally unprofessional.

Her gaze never leaving his back, Celina considered telling him she'd changed her mind about the exam. But her reason for being here was too important for her to turn back now. Still, she was not ready to confide in Reid Prescott. Nor did she want him performing this exam. "I hope you won't be offended," she said stiffly. "But I'm used to Doc and I'd rather wait for him."

Reid breathed a sigh of relief. Turning to face her, he smiled politely. "I understand. I'll tell Glenda." Grabbing this chance for escape, he left, dropping the folder back into the holder on the outside of the door as he went. He'd known Celina Warley would be trouble for him, he thought, as he went in search of Glenda. But he'd never expected the trouble to take the form of an attraction toward the woman.

Celina, also, breathed a sigh of relief and settled back to wait for Doc. But it wasn't Doc who entered next. It was Glenda. Glenda Jones was a happily married woman in her early forties, with three children and a motherly manner. She'd been Doc's nurse-receptionist for the past twenty years and ran his office with an efficient but caring touch. When Celina had become deaf, Glenda had been one of the first to enroll for classes in sign language. She liked to joke that she enjoyed keeping her fingers on the pulse of the community. Celina guessed that this was more than a jest. She was fairly certain that Glenda knew nearly as much about the patients who passed through these offices as Doc did. But, she was also certain that, if this was true, Glenda was discreet. She never talked about what she knew, which was why she'd had this job for so long and why Doc trusted her.

"I'm so sorry about sending Dr. Prescott in," the woman said, signing in large exaggerated motions to give emphasis to her apology. "It wasn't until after I sent him in that Karen told me she'd heard that Julia Johnson had seen him calling on you last evening." Glenda smiled knowingly. "And I'm sure you want to maintain a bit of modesty with a personal relationship developing."

Celina was shocked that people thought Reid was courting her. Then her sense of humor ignited. The good doctor would be even more shocked, she thought. But she couldn't allow this rumor to spread, especially with the plan she had in mind. "Dr. Prescott merely came to see me to apologize for a misunderstanding that occurred yesterday afternoon. There is nothing personal going on between us," Celina told the woman, signing as she spoke to make certain she was clearly understood.

Glenda looked disappointed. "I'm sorry to hear that. You two would make a cute couple."

Celina screwed up her face into a grimace of doubt. She'd given up on finding a man to share her life. And even if she hadn't, Reid Prescott had made it clear he disapproved of her and wanted as little to do with her as possible. "I don't think so," she said firmly.

"Too bad," Glenda replied with a sad shake of her head. Then her manner becoming more businesslike, she added, "I'll send Doc in as soon as he's free."

Watching her leave, Celina wondered what the nurse would think of the reason she'd come to see Doc. She probably wouldn't approve, she decided. Then her shoulders squared. She didn't care what other people thought. This was her decision to make.

"You want to what?" Doc demanded.

Celina had rarely seen Doc lose his composure. But, she guessed this was the first time anyone had made such a request. "I want you to arrange for me to be artificially inseminated," she repeated. "I want to have a child."

"You're twenty-seven. It's not unusual for a woman your age to begin feeling what I've always called the nesting instinct," he said, his voice taking on a more reasoning tone. "However, it is my opinion that finding a husband would be a more appropriate way of dealing with this urge."

Celina faced him calmly. "There is no man in or around Smytheshire I want to marry. And I don't want to leave here. This is my home. I like it here."

"What about your family?" Doc asked, trying another route.

Celina sighed. "I suppose they'll be upset, but I doubt they'll disown me."

Doc was forced to agree. Both the Warleys and the Tuppers were warmhearted people. They would never turn against Celina. "What about your job? There are going to be those who won't think it's appropriate to have an unwed pregnant librarian.''

"As you well know, the library was built by Angus Smythe and operates out of a trust set up by him. The only people who can fire me are the three members of the board set up to oversee that trust. One of them has a daughter who is currently living with a man she isn't married to, and another has a son who got one girl pregnant while he was engaged to another." Her gaze leveled on Doc. "You remember how nervous everyone was when the boy married the first girl while we all waited, hoping the second girl wasn't pregnant, too." She shrugged. "Besides, they can only fire me for dereliction of duty or sexual misconduct. I've always performed my duties well, and I don't see how anyone could call a medical procedure sexual misconduct."

"People label actions to suit their needs," Doc pointed out.

Celina's jaw firmed. "I don't think this town is that vindictive. Look how they treated Emily Sayer. Granted, her family disowned her, but there were others who helped her."

Doc shook his head. "I can see you've got your mind set on this, but I wish you'd give it second thoughts." Even his signing gestures took on the flavor of a plea as he added, "Talk to your grandparents and your aunt Adelle, then come back to see me. If you really want to do this, I want to be the one to see you through it. But I hope you'll reconsider."

Celina read the concern on his face. "I know you're worried about me," she said. "And I'll talk to my grandparents and my aunt. But I'm not going to change my mind." She looked at him pleadingly. "I'm lonely, Doc. I want a child to love and share my life with."

"Promise me you'll talk to your family," he replied, moving his hands forcefully to give command to his words.

Celina held up her hands as if stopping traffic. "All right. All right. I will. I promise."

Celina sat in the rocking chair on her front porch. Her feet were propped up on the railing and she was staring blankly out at the street beyond. She couldn't remember ever feeling this drained. During the afternoon, she'd gone to see both sets of grandparents and her aunt Adelle. All had tried to dissuade her. They'd also said they would stand by her no matter what her decision. She knew, though, that if she went through with the pregnancy it would be hard on her grandparents. Her aunt Adelle would handle it better but even she'd have some difficulty coping with the whispers of disapproval that were bound to go on behind Celina's back. She didn't want to hurt her family or cause them any discomfort, but they didn't understand how alone and isolated she felt.

A man coming down the sidewalk caught her attention. It was Reid Prescott.

Reid couldn't believe he'd once again found his way to Celina Warley's doorstep. But as he and Doc had explained to all their patients, they were running their practice as a joint venture. They discussed all their cases so that if Reid didn't remain, Doc wouldn't have to step in cold with the patients Reid had been seeing; if Reid did take over the practice, he wouldn't have to step in cold with the patients Doc had been seeing. In particular, they made it a point to discuss any problem or unusual cases. And so, during dinner, Doc had told Reid about Celina's request and asked him to try to talk some sense into her. "If Doc couldn't talk her out of this, I don't know what I can do," Reid muttered under his breath. Still, he'd said he would try.

"Good evening," he signed as he opened the white picket gate and started up the walk toward her porch.

She didn't have to guess why he was there. She was sure Doc had sent him. "Depends," she replied. "If you mean the weather, then you're correct."

Coming to a halt at the top of the porch steps, he leaned against the nearest column and studied her. "Had a tough afternoon?" he asked, already knowing the answer from the tired lines on her face.

She grimaced. "You could say that."

He'd been wondering how he was going to broach the reason he was there. Bluntly, he decided. "As Doc and I have explained to our patients, we consult on all our cases. He told me what you asked him to do."

She frowned at him. "And I suppose you disapprove too."

"I think you've chosen a very difficult path," he replied slowly, signing as he spoke.

"Life is full of difficult paths."

Reid grinned. "I didn't realize you were a philosopher."

Celina hadn't thought of Reid Prescott as a handsome man. His features were proportioned so that they fitted well together but there was a roughness, an angularity about them that produced a somewhat harsh countenance. But when he smiled, the lines of his face softened and she had to admit he looked rather appealing. *I'm more tired than I thought,* she mused, jerking her gaze away from him.

Reid saw her turn away. Apparently, she didn't want to talk to him. Well, he wasn't all that thrilled about being here, either. But he'd promised Doc he'd try to talk some sense into her. And, he admitted, he didn't want to see her make a mistake that would bring her pain. Leaning forward, he tapped her on the shoulder to regain her attention.

Celina swung her gaze back to him as the feel of the light contact lingered on her skin.

"Don't you think it might be wise for you to find a husband first?" he signed.

She'd had this same conversation with both sets of grandparents and her aunt Adelle. With them, she had simply explained that no man here in Smytheshire interested her. But now her nerves were near the snapping point. She was in no mood to be coy. "I don't know if it's because I'm deaf, but the men who've come courting have fallen into two categories—those who want to protect me until I feel so smothered I can't breathe and those who act as if I should be grateful for any time they are willing to give me. I have no intention of tying myself to either." Her jaw tensed. "If I could," she signed, her hands moving with sharp bursts of energy, "I would have this child without involving any man, but since there is only one being who is capable of granting that wish and he doesn't do it on request, I've decided to use the next best method."

It occurred to Reid that he'd never seen a woman look so determined.

"Evening," a female voice called out.

Reid turned toward the street. "Evening," he called back.

Celina had seen Reid's attention shift to the street and looked to see why. Julia and Paul Johnson were out for their regular evening stroll. The moment Julia saw her looking their way, she waved and the smile on her face broadened. Celina forced a smile and waved back. Then, the smile vanishing, she turned back to Reid Prescott. She'd told him more than she'd ever planned to tell anyone. Now she felt embarrassed and just wanted him to go away. "For the sake of your reputation, I'd suggest you leave," she said.

Reid regarded her questioningly. "My reputation?"

"This makes two evenings in a row the Johnsons have seen you here," Celina replied. "That kind of news travels fast. I told Glenda that last night you were here on official business. But she might not believe me if I used that to explain this visit, too. Once I'm pregnant, there could be rumors that you're the father."

Reid knew when he was being told to get lost. He didn't want any rumors circulating that suggested misbehavior on his part, either. That would be detrimental to his career. Besides, he didn't see any reason for prolonging this conversation. Celina Warley's mind was made up, and it was his opinion that nothing was going to change it. "I hope you'll give this matter a little more thought before you make a final decision," he signed. Then, adding a good-evening, he left.

As he passed through her gate, the loneliness she'd been feeling so strongly for the past months descended on Celina again. This time it was even more pronounced. "I have given this matter a great deal of thought," she murmured, her features hardening with resolve.

Chapter Three

The next evening, Celina found herself seated in one of the two large wing chairs in Doc's living room. Doc had dropped into the library that afternoon and asked her to come to his home for dinner. Actually, it had been more of an order than an invitation. But she'd been more than willing to agree. Both grandmothers and her Aunt Adelle had been on her doorstep before breakfast this morning. She didn't relish an evening with the grandfathers and Aunt Adelle coming by to try to persuade her to change her mind.

When she'd arrived at Doc's, it was obvious Reid Prescott hadn't been expecting her. There had been surprise on his face when he'd answered her knock on the door.

Doc had sent Doreen Troy, his housekeeper and cook, home as soon as she'd finished preparing the meal. Then he'd set it on the table himself. During dinner, Reid had tried to make light conversation, clearly uncertain of what Doc had in mind.

As the meal had progressed, Celina had grown more and more uneasy. She'd kept glancing from Doc, who seemed to be scrutinizing her, to Reid, who was trying to politely ignore her.

But dinner was over, and Reid was seated near her in the twin chair next to the one in which she sat. Doc was standing in front of them, regarding them with a decisive set to his jaw.

"I have something to say to the two of you," Doc began, abruptly breaking the silence that had fallen after they'd entered the living room and Celina and Reid had taken the seats he'd indicated. Keeping his face toward Celina and signing as he spoke, he continued, "I've given your request a great deal of thought. Both of your grandmothers and your aunt Adelle came in to see me today. And I received calls from your grandfathers. Despite the fact that we're all worried that you'll regret your decision, your mind appears to be firmly set."

Celina nodded.

Doc shook his head as if he thought this was folly. Then, his expression remaining grim, he turned toward Reid. He continued to sign as he spoke so that Celina would know what he was saying. "When Brian Smythe and I talked about finding a new doctor to take my place, he was very clear that he wanted someone settled. To him that means a family man. He wasn't happy when I chose to ask you to come here on a trial basis. But I pointed out that you were only thirty and had been devoting all your time to learning to be the best doctor you could be. I told him that it was my opinion that you simply hadn't had time to find a wife. I also hinted that you would feel even more a part of the community if you married someone here. However, since you've been here, we've discussed marriage and you've made it clear it is not an institution in which you wish to enroll. This poses a problem. I thought your abilities as a doctor might convince Brian to change his mind about insisting that the new doctor be a married man. But he hasn't. Of course, you are always free to set up a practice on your own, but you would have to buy all your equipment and find new office space. And you'd be a country doctor. That is not a lucrative practice. It would take you years to pay off your debts.''

"Then I guess I'd better pack my bags and be on my way," Reid said tersely. "No sense in wasting any more of your time or mine."

Celina couldn't catch every word Reid was saying. He was speaking to Doc and he wasn't signing. But from the expression on his face, she was fairly certain he was letting Doc know that he wasn't going to let anyone dictate how he should live his life.

"Wait," Doc ordered when Reid started to rise, obviously intending to leave. "I haven't finished."

Settling back into his chair, Reid regarded Doc guardedly. An inkling of where this little speech might be going occurred to him. But he couldn't believe Doc would propose such a ridiculous solution. Still...

"The way I see it, you're both caught in dilemmas," Doc continued, his attention shifting back to Celina to make certain she could see what he was saying. "You could help each other out by getting married. That way, Celina, you would have a husband, which would save your grandparents a great deal of agony and worry. And—" his gaze narrowed on her

"—you need to think about your child. Having a flesh-and-blood father for him or her to see will be a lot easier than having to explain that your male counterpart started out as an icicle." His gaze shifted to Reid. "And you would have a wife who is tied into our community. When you negotiate your contract with Smythe, you can insist on at least a twenty-year lease, saying you want to feel secure. Then, even if the marriage doesn't work, that will give you plenty of time to build up a practice and put money aside to establish your own office if the Smythes insist on finding someone else."

Celina stared at Doc in a shocked silence. She couldn't believe he'd actually made this suggestion.

Reid mentally shook his head in astonishment. He'd been right about where Doc was leading, but he was still finding it difficult to believe the old man would offer this solution.

"At least think about what I've said," Doc pleaded, breaking the heavy silence that had descended over the room. "I'm going for a walk."

For a long moment after Doc had gone Celina sat staring at the doorway. Finally, knowing she had to say something to Reid, she turned toward him. He had a bemused expression on his face as he continued to look in the direction Doc had gone. "It's an absurd suggestion," she said.

Reid turned toward her. "Preposterous," he agreed.

Celina suddenly found herself recalling the electric sensation of his touch and wondering how it would feel to be in his embrace. *In his arms is the last place I belong and the very last place he would want me to be,* she chided herself. "I think I'll be going home now," she said, rising as she spoke.

Reid merely nodded. But as he watched her leave, he couldn't help thinking she had a damnably enticing swing to her hips. But marriage to Celina Warley was out of the question. Marriage for him at all was out of the question.

For another long moment he continued to sit and stare at the space Doc had occupied. "Preposterous," he repeated. His gaze shifted toward the window, and the darkness beyond. A sudden anxiety washed over him. Celina's car hadn't been parked outside. That meant she'd walked over to Doc's. Now she was walking home alone.

"She's perfectly safe in this town," he told himself. But he'd lived in New York too long. In one lithe movement, he rose to his feet, and jogged out of the house.

Celina gasped when she felt the tap on her shoulder. She'd been so intently telling herself that Doc's suggestion was absurd, she was barely conscious of the rest of the world around her. Coming to an abrupt stop, she turned to discover Reid Prescott had joined her.

"I thought I should do the polite thing and walk you home," he said.

The only light they had was that cast by the porch lights and the moon, but she managed to lip-read the words "polite" and "walk you home." For a moment, when she'd discovered he'd followed her, she'd felt a surge of excitement. But the grim expression on his face made her feel as if he was performing a duty he considered an imposition. "That really isn't necessary," she replied.

"Yes, it is," he insisted. "For my own peace of mind, I'm going to see you to your door."

A fresh protest formed on her lips, but the set of his jaw told her that arguing would be useless. Giving a shrug, she said, "Suit yourself," then resumed walking down the street.

As he fell into step beside her, she couldn't stop herself from glancing covertly at him. His frown grated on her nerves. She was just about to stop and order him to go home when it occurred to her that at least a portion of his irritation might be due to her curt response to Doc's suggestion. Of course, he'd agreed, but she had been rather harsh.

"I want you to know that I don't think you're terrible husband material," she said.

Glancing toward her, Reid cocked an eyebrow as if he wasn't quite certain this was a compliment, while inwardly, he admitted that he had been insulted by her brusque response to Doc's suggestion. He also admitted it was silly of him to feel that way, because he agreed that a marriage between the two of them was ridiculous. *Guess my ego's a little easier to damage than I thought,* he mused wryly.

Celina realized she hadn't phrased her apology in a particularly flattering manner. "I'm sure you'd make some woman a wonderful husband," she added.

"Thanks," he signed, then returned his attention to the sidewalk ahead.

Celina felt piqued. She'd apologized to him, and now it seemed only fair for him to apologize to her in return. After all, he'd made marriage to her sound like a fate worse than death—"preposterous," he'd said. *I don't really care what he thinks of me,* she assured herself. Still, she picked up her pace, wanting to get home and be rid of his company as quickly as possible. Reaching her gate, she paused, bade him a quick dismissive goodbye, and started up the walk toward her house.

She is kind of cute when she's irritated, Reid thought. When she'd picked up her pace, he'd guessed why. And, he admitted, he was pleased to know that she seemed to care what he thought of her. Until this moment, he'd been certain that if she didn't simply dislike him, she was at best indifferent to him.

He followed her up to her porch, and caught her arm, stopping her before she could enter the house. Releasing her arm, he began to sign as he spoke. "I have something I want to say. I waited until we reached your house so that we would have light so you could see my words," he explained. "It's my opinion that you would make a man as good a wife as any other woman. But I'm not interested in marriage. My mother has been married four times and my father has been married twice and divorced twice. My family albums are arranged by marriages and divorces instead of by years. It's my belief that people fall in love with each other's little quirks and then after a few years, or even after a few months, those same little quirks are driving them crazy. Doc claims that marriage can be a very rewarding and fulfilling arrangement. I suppose he could be right. On the other hand, those marriages that look so great could simply be surface shows, and beneath their companionable smiles both people are miserable. Doc says I'm a cynic. But I refuse to enter the fray."

Celina told herself it shouldn't make any difference, but she was pleased to know that his rejection of Doc's suggestion hadn't been because he considered her totally unacceptable as a wife. "Doc's right. You are a cynic," she replied, a hint of a smile playing at the corners of her mouth.

He grinned wryly. "I know. But I'm a happy one."

"Then I'm happy for you," she replied.

His expression became serious. "And I hope whatever decision you make regarding a child makes you happy."

"Thanks," she signed. Her legs felt suddenly weak as she gazed up into his blue eyes. A warmth still lingered on her arm where he'd grasped it to stop her from entering the house. Again, she found herself wondering what it would be like to be in his arms. *That's something you're never going to find out,* she reminded herself, jerking her gaze away. "Good night," she said, fitting her key into the lock.

He waited until she was inside. Then he said a quick good-night and turned away. As the door closed behind him, Reid drew a sharp breath. For a moment, when she'd looked at him just before unlocking her door, he'd again felt himself getting lost in those brown eyes of hers. "I'm more aware of her than I usually am of a woman because I'm concerned about her," he murmured under his breath as he walked toward the street. "I don't think she really understands how difficult her life will become if she goes through with this notion of having a child out of wedlock."

Later that night Celina lay in bed staring into the darkness surrounding her. She was too restless to sleep. Maybe she was being unfair to her family. She loved them and didn't want to make them suffer the gossip that was bound to occur if she went through with her plan. And maybe she was being unfair to the child. Josh Sayer's life hadn't been easy. She'd seen the taunts from other children. . . .

A tear trickled from her eye. She was tired of being so alone. She rubbed her temples as the mild headache that had been tormenting her grew stronger. Maybe she should reconsider finding a husband. Possible choices paraded through her mind. "I may be lonely but I'm not desperate," she muttered as she rejected each in turn. Then Reid Prescott filled her inner vision. "He's not available," she reminded herself. Totally exhausted, she fell into a restless sleep.

Reid Prescott yawned as he drove down Oak Street. Glancing at his watch, he saw it was nearly midnight. He'd received a call from Bruce Stuart a little earlier. Olivia, Bruce's wife of over sixty years, had been complaining of heart palpitations. Reid had heard the panic in the elderly man's voice and immediately promised to come by. By the time he got there, her heart rhythm was normal again. He'd stayed awhile to make certain they were both fine, told Bruce he'd stop by to see them the next morning, then left.

But instead of taking the shortest route back to Doc's place, he found himself driving by Celina Warley's. Her lights were out. He guessed she was sleeping. He pictured her snuggled in bed and a fire ignited within him. He scowled.

Admittedly, he conceded, marriage worked for some people. Bruce and Olivia Stuart were proof of that. He envied them their companionship, too. But they were the exception, not the rule, he reminded himself, recalling the statistics on divorce. And, even if the statistics weren't so depressing, marriage wasn't for him. He had a busy life, and he wasn't interested in adjusting his time to accommodate another person's life. "There isn't that much adjusting I could do, anyway," he added grimly. Being a general practitioner here in Smytheshire would require him to be available at any hour of any day.

As he pulled into Doc's driveway, Celina's image again filled his mind. "I hope she takes Doc's advice and finds a husband," he said. His jaw firmed. "But it isn't going to be me."

Celina had just poured her first cup of coffee the next morning when the light in her kitchen blinked off and on a couple of times. Like several of the lights throughout the house, it had been wired to the front doorbell so that it blinked when someone rang. She groaned at the thought of another early morning confrontation with her grandmothers. Reluctantly she walked to her front door. But when she opened it, she discovered her grandfathers there, instead. Both were quiet men who were slow to judge other people harshly and rarely interfered in the lives of their children or grandchildren. "Come in," she said, stepping aside to allow them to enter.

"Morning, girl," Ralph Tupper said, giving his granddaughter a hug.

"Morning," Amos Warley parroted as he waited his turn to give her a hug.

As she returned their hugs, the uneasiness she read in their faces caused Celina to feel guilty. She didn't like upsetting the members of her family. They'd always treated her so well.

"Neither of us is much good at this signing business," Ralph Tupper said, awkwardly gesturing his way through the sentence. "And we didn't want to rely only on your lip-reading. We wanted to be sure you understood exactly what we have to say." He nodded toward an envelope Amos Warley was extending toward her. "So we wrote you a letter."

"I'm sorry. I know I've upset you," Celina said with deep apology.

Ralph Tupper wrapped his arms around his granddaughter and gave her another hug. Stepping back, he said slowly, pronouncing each word distinctly, "You do what you feel you have to do."

Amos tapped her on the shoulder. "Everyone is entitled to their own life," he said with the same slow deliberation. Clearly wanting her to understand, he also attempted to sign the words as he spoke.

"Thank you, both," she said, tears glistening in her eyes.

"Got to go take care of my crops now," Amos said. He touched her cheek gently. "You take care of yourself, girl."

Ralph stepped up and gave her a hug, then followed Amos out.

Watching them climb into Amos's truck and drive off, Celina felt her tears well up more. She was lucky to have men like her grandfathers in her life. They were dependable caring men. *Like the man I'd hoped to marry.* But that man had never crossed her path. Again the image of Reid Prescott flashed into her mind. *He's a doctor, so he must care about people, and Doc thinks he's dependable. But he doesn't want to get married,* she reminded herself. *And even if he ever does, he won't choose me.*

Carrying the letter into the kitchen, she sat down at the table and read it. In it, her grandfathers expressed their love then went on to state bluntly that they thought she might be asking for more trouble than she knew if she went through with her decision. They ended the letter by saying that no matter what she chose to do, they would stand by her and support and love her.

"It's becoming so complicated," she muttered, brushing away a stream of tears. "I don't want to hurt anyone or cause anyone any grief."

Later as she dressed for work, she had to admit that her resolve was weakening. "Maybe I should look around for a husband one more time," she said with a heavy sigh.

Reid sat drinking his morning coffee on Doc's front porch. The soft warmth of summer enveloped him as he breathed in the sweet-smelling air. It was nice here in this quiet little town nestled in the mountains of Massachusetts. He'd lived in cities most of his life. But this was the kind of place he'd always fantasized about living in. And the kind of family practice Doc had was the kind of practice he wanted.

But he was still paying off medical-school debts. He had no money to set up his own practice. If he didn't get the lease on Doc's offices, he'd have to find another family practitioner who wanted a junior partner. A spark of irritation flashed in his eyes and he was forced to admit he didn't like the idea of being under someone's thumb. He liked his independence.

A frown spread over his face, emphasizing the tired lines left by a restless night. He knew Doc had been telling the truth when he'd said that Brian Smythe wanted a married man as the new doctor for Smythe-shire. Reid recalled being invited to Brian Smythe's home for dinner a couple of weeks ago. Brian had in-

formed Reid that Doc was pleased with the work Reid
was doing. But Brian had been blunt about his doubts
regarding an unmarried doctor. "Too much leeway for
rumors and angry husbands," he'd said. "And an
unmarried man is more apt to be unsettled. Just when
people begin to think of you as a part of the community, you might get the notion to just up and move
away. Or you might fall in love with a woman who
wouldn't want to live in such a quiet isolated place. I
wouldn't want us to suddenly have to go looking for a
doctor and not have time to make a thorough search."

Reid had assured him that he was totally professional with all his patients and that he would not
abruptly leave their small community without ade-
quate medical care. At the time, he hadn't been able
to tell if his assurances had been enough for the elder
Smythe. Now he knew they hadn't been. It was clear
that Doc had been relaying a message from Brian
Smythe last night.

Leaning back in his chair with his feet propped up
on the rail, Reid pictured Celina Warley. He couldn't
deny that he found her desirable. The truth was he felt
one heck of a strong attraction toward the woman; he
was still surprised by the heat she stirred in him. But a
wife?

"Heard you've been seeing a lot of our librarian,"
a female voice broke into his thoughts.

Reid looked in the direction from which the voice
had come and saw Doreen Troy, Doc's housekeeper,
climbing the porch steps. Doreen was in her midfif-
ties and had two grown children. Her husband, Wal-
lis, owned and operated the only barber shop in
Smytheshire. Doreen was a lifelong resident of Smytheshire and knew everyone. Reid would not classify her

as a gossip but there was a sparkle of curiosity in her eyes this morning. It occurred to him that if Celina did go ahead with her planned pregnancy, no matter how firmly Doc, he and Celina told people he wasn't the father, there would be rumors. And that was sure to ruin any shred of a chance that Brian Smythe might change his mind and allow Reid to take over Doc's practice. "I've been consulting with her about a patient," he replied curtly.

Doreen looked disappointed. "Too bad. I've always liked Celina. Been hoping she'd find herself a nice man and marry. I know that would take a lot of worry off her grandparents' shoulders. They'd feel more secure knowing she had a man to look after her. 'Course it's really us women who take care of you men the majority of the time. But it's nice to have a strong shoulder to lean on when it's needed." Having made this observation, Doreen gave a nod as if adding a final emphasis to her words, then went inside.

"It would seem that, if I'm going to stay in town, I'm going to have to marry Celina Warley," Reid muttered.

Chapter Four

Celina looked at the book she'd just returned to the shelf. It was a fiction selection. But instead of shelving it by the author's name, she'd used the first word in the title. "At least I was in the right section of the library," she said to herself as she pulled the book out and carried it to the proper shelf. As she shoved it into its place, she wondered how many other books she'd incorrectly shelved this morning.

Deciding to stop before she did any more damage, she pushed the book-laden cart toward the front desk. She'd been trying to concentrate on her work, instead of going over the pros and cons of continuing with her plan to have a child. But the words in the letter from her grandfathers had been playing through her mind, along with the anxious faces of her grandmothers and her Aunt Adelle. Maybe they were right. She had them and her work. There was no reason for her to feel so terribly lonely. Maybe this wanting to have a child was just a phase she was going through, she thought. Maybe, with time, it would just fade away.

Nearing the desk, she saw Ellen Vough, the twenty-five-year-old second-grade teacher, there. Brenda Norwood, Celina's assistant, was with her and both were watching Celina.

"Would you shelve the rest of these books?" Celina directed Brenda as she reached the two women.

Brenda nodded, then tossing a knowing smile over her shoulder at Ellen, she pushed off with the book-laden cart.

Ellen grinned as she scribbled a message on the pad of paper on the desk. Looking down at it, Celina read, "It's Dr. Prescott, isn't it? Men are always causing women to go around muttering to themselves."

It's a wonder the gossip doesn't already have Reid Prescott and me engaged, Celina thought dryly. She forced a smile. "Dr. Prescott and I are merely acquaintances," she said firmly. "My muttering has nothing to do with him."

Ellen flushed with embarrassment. "Sorry, I didn't mean to pry," she wrote hurriedly.

"It's all right," Celina assured her as she took the books Ellen had chosen and began processing them. But when she'd finished and pushed the books back toward the young woman, she noticed Ellen hesitate and an uneasiness spread over the teacher's face.

Chewing self-consciously on her bottom lip, Ellen scribbled another note. A glow of pleasure reddened her cheeks as she turned the paper toward Celina.

"I've just discovered that I'm pregnant." Celina read. "And I'm happy but nervous. Doc has assured me that everything is fine. But this is my first, and I was wondering if you'd mind touching me for luck and to reassure me that everything is all right."

Celina had grown used to requests like this. She wondered what Reid Prescott would think if he knew. He'd probably blow another gasket, she mused. "As long as you promise me you'll continue to see Doc," Celina stipulated.

"Of course," Ellen assured her, then suddenly realizing she'd spoken, instead of written the words, she reached for the pad of paper.

"I understood," Celina said, reaching out to stop her.

Ellen flushed again this time with embarrassment as she released the pencil and straightened.

Glancing around and noting there was no one other than the two of them and Brenda in the library at the moment, Celina rounded the desk. Gently she placed a hand flat on Ellen's lower abdomen. A sense of well-being and joy flowed through her. "Your baby is fine," she said, breaking the contact. Her expression intensely serious, she added, "But you must take good care of yourself and see Doc regularly."

"Sounds like sound advice to me."

Celina saw Ellen jerk around. Looking past the woman's shoulder, she saw Reid Prescott approaching them. There was impatient reprimand on his face.

Ellen flushed under his curt scrutiny. "I'd better be going," she said, grabbing up her books and striding toward the door.

'Practicing medicine without a license again, I see,' Reid signed as soon as he and Celina were alone.

"I wasn't 'practicing medicine,'" she replied, meeting his gaze levelly. "It's natural for women to be

nervous about their pregnancies. So they come to me
for some reassurance.''

''And then they can use your reassurance to tell
themselves they don't need to see a doctor,'' he
growled, signing the words with sharp angry motions
as he spoke.

''No!'' She glared at him. ''I always insist they see
Doc. And as you've already discovered, I tell him who
has been to see me.'' Then deciding to make certain he
knew her complete arrangement with Doc, she added,
''If I've sensed anything wrong with the baby, I tell
Doc so he can run a few extra tests and keep a closer
eye on the mother.'' It occurred to her that if Reid
Prescott did take over Doc's practice, he probably
wouldn't listen to her. But she'd have to tell him, anyway, she knew. Her conscience would make her.

''He told me that was the way you two worked,''
Reid replied. He raked a hand through his hair. He
hadn't come in here to fight with this woman. However, my reason for being here is ludicrous, he told
himself. But even as the temptation to turn and leave
swept through him, he found himself reasoning that
her agreement to his proposal would ensure his being
able to keep an eye on her and make certain she didn't
endanger any of the residents of Smytheshire. His jaw
hardened with resolve. ''Is there someplace here we
can talk privately?''

Celina glanced around to make certain no patrons
who needed her help had entered, then she led the way
toward her office in the back.

Reid closed the door to ensure their privacy, then
turned to face her. She was watching him with a
guarded air, as if she wasn't certain if he were friend
or foe. She's never going to agree to this, he told him-

self, feeling more like a fool with each passing moment. "I've been thinking about what Doc said last night," he began, both signing and speaking.

Celina saw his tenseness in his gestures and on his face. Clearly he was uneasy about being there, she thought, wondering why anything Doc had said would cause him to come see her.

Reid fought the urge to pace. "My parents have always married for love. Combined, they've been to the altar six times. Five of those unions were unsuccessful. I don't know how my mother's current marriage will work out but I figure it won't last, either." Reid paused. *This is crazy,* he told himself again.

A nervousness spread through Celina as he stood regarding her in a curt silence. "Maybe they don't understand what love really is," she said, feeling the need to make some sort of response. "Maybe they get caught up in the fantasy of what love is. They think marriage should be all wine and roses. They don't understand that relationships must have a practical side." *You're babbling,* she chided herself, and clamped her mouth shut.

Reid nodded. "Yes, a practical side." Reminding himself that he'd thought this out thoroughly before coming here and concluded that what he was about to propose was a reasonable solution to his problems and hers, he continued stiffly, "That's why I'm here. I've been thinking about the practical side of marriage. It's occurred to me that if both people are benefiting in a practical way from the union, then it has a chance of working. For my part, I want a practice like the one Doc has and I want to remain here in Smytheshire. But, at the present time, I can't afford to open my own office. To remain here, I need the Smythes' lease. You

want a child. If you have a husband, you can achieve
that goal and still maintain your current comfortable
position within the community, and your family will
not suffer any gossip. I have some medical-school
debts to repay, but eventually I'll make a decent living and can offer any children we might have financial security."

Hoping she looked casual, Celina leaned back
against her desk. The truth was she needed the support. She wasn't sure her legs would hold her. His initial reaction to Doc's suggestion had convinced her he
would never consider marriage to her. Yet it seemed
that was exactly what he was doing. "Are you pro-
posing?" she asked, feeling the need to assure herself
she had understood correctly.

"Like Doc said, marriage is a practical solution to
both our problems," he replied, feeling like a complete idiot as he read the shocked disbelief on her face.
He and Doc might both think this was a reasonable
way to resolve their respective dilemmas, but clearly
Celina did not. Pride caused his back to stiffen.
"However, it appears you don't agree. Sorry I took up
your time."

Celina had been watching him, almost afraid to
move or even breath. He was right about her family.
A husband would please them. Having a husband
would also make life easier for her. And, she had to
admit, the thought of him being that husband was not
disagreeable. As he turned toward the door, a strength
born of pure nervousness flowed through her.
Abruptly she stepped forward and laid a restraining
hand on his arm. A current of heated excitement traveled through her and she quickly released him. "We
probably have less than a fifty-fifty chance of making

a marriage work," she said. "But you're right about my family. And a flesh-and-blood father would be easier to explain to a child than a defrosted ice cube in a syringe."

The hesitation Reid saw in her eyes irritated him. After all, considering her alternatives, he wasn't such a bad choice for a husband. Then he laughed at himself. He and Celina Warley weren't even friends. They were barely acquaintances. It was surprising she wasn't either laughing at him or throwing him out of her office. They'd both probably be better off if she decided to choose one of those two reactions. Still, he heard himself saying, "Statistically, a fifty-fifty chance is better than average where marriages in this country are concerned."

"You're right," she conceded, trying to think clearly. But her heart was pounding so rapidly she was beginning to feel light-headed. "We might as well give it a try." She had to fight back a gasp as she realized what she'd said.

Reid was surprised by the rush of pleasure her acceptance caused. He told himself it was merely due to his male need to win and to the fact that this marriage would help him accomplish his goal. "I'm glad you agree," he said, maintaining a businesslike facade. The desire to start making the arrangements before she could change her mind was strong, but he had patients he had to see. "Now, I've got to get back to the office," he continued in the same impersonal tones. "I'll come by around six and take you out to dinner. Afterward, we can set a date for a wedding."

"Six," Celina repeated.

Reid nodded, then left.

Her legs again threatening to buckle, Celina sank into a nearby chair. She'd just agreed to marry a man who was practically a stranger. "Well, I was going to have a baby by a man I didn't even know," she reminded herself. Of course, she hadn't been going to share that man's bed. Reid Prescott's image loomed in her mind. A fresh wave of nervousness swept over her.

The blinking of the light above her office door caught her eye. Her legs still felt shaky as she rose to see who was there. But before she'd taken a step, the door opened and her aunt entered. Adelle Warley was in her fifties, a little on the plump side with a pleasantly featured face. She'd never married. The story was that in her youth she'd been engaged to a young man who was in the military. He'd been killed and she'd never found anyone else. Instead, she'd started a business as a seamstress. Now the lower floor of her home housed the only dress shop in town, and she made a reasonably good living selling both off-the-rack clothes and those she made herself. "I saw Dr. Prescott leaving as I was coming in," Adelle said, closing the door behind her. As if still worried that they might be overheard, she stopped speaking aloud and began only signing. "Have you actually arranged to purchase the frozen daddy-sicle?"

Celina scowled at her aunt's attempt at humor. "No." She started to tell her aunt about Reid Prescott's proposal but said, instead, "I've decided to consider other options first."

Adelle studied her niece anxiously. "I can't honestly say I understand this need of yours to have a child. I've been perfectly happy on my own, unencumbered, free to come and go as I wish with no other person to tie my schedule to. Of course, I've always been the one the other members of our family seek out when they're troubled or worried and need to talk. Needless to say my doorstep has rarely been empty. And I've had you and the others to love and fuss over. However, we must all march to the beat of our own drummer." A plea entered her eyes. "But I do hope that a husband is one of the options you're considering."

Again Celina considered telling her aunt that she'd just agreed to marry Reid Prescott and again she didn't. "It is," was all she said.

"I know you're tired of hearing people say this," Adelle continued, signing and speaking slowly to make certain Celina caught every word, "but we love you and we want the best for you. If you go through with this plan to be a single parent, we'll stick by you. But there'll be whispers behind your back and life won't be easy for your child. There are always a few cruel children who enjoy tormenting others. A child without a father will be fodder for them. And there'll be a few narrow-minded adults who'll always look down on you and your offspring. That's the real world."

"I know," Celina replied. Those were precisely the reasons her resolve had weakened. But she was tired of having this same conversation with members of her family. She glanced at her watch. "I've got the sixth-grade class from the school coming to do research in fifteen minutes," she said.

Adelle held up her hand. "I know when I'm being thrown out." Giving Celina an encouraging smile to let her know that she wasn't offended, she hugged her niece tightly, then left.

Celina drew a terse breath. She hadn't told her aunt about her engagement to Reid Prescott because it didn't seem real. He hadn't even kissed her. A sudden apprehension filled her. What if they weren't physically compatible?

She issued a moan as her head began to pound. "I'll think about this later," she promised herself as she rose and left her office.

Later had arrived, and she'd been thinking about nothing else but Reid Prescott's proposal for the past two hours. Pacing her living-room floor, she looked out the front window. He was coming up the walk. Her gaze traveled over him from his broad shoulders to the sturdy columns of his legs. A feminine appreciation of his physique caused her blood to race faster, and her worries about their physical incompatibility diminished somewhat

But as he came nearer and she saw the grim expression on his face, her blood slowed and a coolness descended over her. "He's changed his mind," she murmured, experiencing a sharp jab of disappointment. Pride kept her expression indifferent as she met him at the door.

Reid's nerves were on a brittle edge. All day he'd been waiting for someone to come in and say something to him about his engagement. It had been like waiting for the second shoe to fall. But it hadn't. "Since you obviously haven't told anyone about our engagement, can I assume you've changed your mind?" he asked the moment he was inside. He'd considered a less blunt way of broaching this question, but he wasn't in the mood for a subtle approach.

Buying a moment's time before she answered, Celina studied him. His expression was shuttered. She couldn't tell if he cared whether or not she might have changed her mind. "I didn't tell anyone because I thought I should give you a day to think about your proposal," she replied. Then honesty forced her to admit, "And I wanted some time to think about us, too."

Reid felt irked. He knew it was irrational to be angry with her. She was behaving in a very reasonable manner. It was his male ego again, he mocked himself. "And now that you've had time to think, what's your decision?"

Until that moment, she hadn't been certain what she would say. But as she'd watched his hands moving, the thought of them touching her had caused the embers of desire to begin to glow within her. "I've decided it would be better to have a child with a husband than to have a child without one," she replied.

A satisfied smile played at the corners of his mouth. "Good."

Celina was startled that he seemed honestly pleased by her acceptance. "You really think we can make this marriage work?" she said, her surprise at his confidence clearly visible.

"What I believe is that we can hold it together long enough to achieve our goals," he answered.

"A practical couple in a practical marriage," she observed dryly. To cover a sudden flood of doubt, she smiled crookedly. "A perfect solution for both of us."

Reid liked her smile. It had a sort of mischievous quality. "Together we stand," he said, signing with exaggerated gestures.

Excitement mingled with fear within Celina. *Think of this as an adventure,* she ordered herself. "Or together we fall," she added.

Reid experienced an unexpected sense of camaraderie with this brown-eyed woman. "And now to begin our courtship." He swirled his hand in a flowery gesture at the end of this pronouncement. "I've made reservations at Marigold Wainwright's place for us—a table for two by the front window."

Celina grinned nervously as she accepted his proffered arm. Marigold ran a big old-fashioned country inn on the outskirts of town. In the summer she had hikers and fishermen staying there. In the winter, the skiers came. Her food was considered a culinary delight by everyone who had ever eaten there. For that reason, all year round her dining room was packed with locals, as well as inn guests. "A very good choice to both eat and be seen," she said as she climbed into his car,

He nodded his agreement as he closed the door.

Dinner went well, Celina thought a couple hours later as she finished her coffee. They'd talked about the food, the weather, books, television shows and sports they both enjoyed. They did, in fact, for all appearances seem to be a couple out on their first date, getting to know one another. They had also been noticed. In addition to the several locals who had stopped by their table to exchange quick hellos, Marigold herself had left her kitchen to come and ask how they were enjoying their dinner.

"By tomorrow, our date should be news all over town," Celina said as she and Reid entered her living room a little later.

"How long do you think this courtship should go on before we announce our engagement?" he asked when they were both seated, Reid on the couch and Celina in a nearby chair.

A fresh wave of nervousness swept over her. Pushing it aside, she said, "Grandma Tupper said she and my grandfather got engaged a week after they started dating. My grandfather says he knew she was the wife for him the first time he laid eyes on her. It just took him a few days to convince her of that. Grandma and Grandpa Warley were high-school sweethearts. They'd promised their parents they wouldn't marry until they'd gotten their diplomas, so they went together for nearly three years before they got married. My parents dated for a couple of months, broke up, then got back together a couple of weeks later and got engaged a month after that."

As he sat watching her, Reid felt a growing impatience to get to know her in a physical way. He admitted to himself he'd had a difficult time all evening keeping his distance. *I've been without a woman's company much too long,* he decided. Aloud he said, "Since we both know what we want, there's no reason to delay the wedding any longer than necessary. I suggest we follow your grandfather and grandmother Tupper's example. This makes the fourth day in a row I've been here at your home. We'll wait another week, then make our engagement official."

This time it was a tidal-wave surge of nervousness that washed over her. Resolutely ignoring it, Celina said, "That's fine with me."

"Do you want a big wedding or a small one?" he signed.

Before she'd given up on finding a husband, Celina had thought about the kind of wedding she wanted. "I'd like to be married in church in my mother's wedding gown," she replied. "And I'd like my family to be there. Other than that, I really don't care."

Reid drew a breath of relief. He'd hoped she wouldn't want a large elaborate wedding. Celina was proving to be a very reasonable woman, he thought. "We'll keep it a family affair, then," he said. "I'll invite my parents and ask Doc to be my best man."

Celina felt the food she'd eaten forming a lump in her stomach. They were actually making plans for a wedding. She knew she'd agreed to marry him, but it occurred to her again that she barely knew him. *He's a decent man or Doc wouldn't have suggested this marriage,* she assured herself. Besides, it wasn't as if they were really going to share their lives. He was simply going to sire the children she wanted, and she was going to be the wife he needed to get the lease from the Smythes.

Movement began to register on her brain pulling her mind away from this inner bout of frantic rationalization. Reid was speaking and signing to her. She caught the words "going" and "have a busy day tomorrow." Then she saw him rise.

Getting to her feet, also, she accompanied him to the door.

As he paused to say good-night, Reid knew he was going to kiss her. The impatience he'd been feeling had been building too long. *I'll probably be disappointed,* he told himself. And that would be for the best. He didn't like being so strongly attracted to her. *It's just a physical urge,* he mocked, dismissing the uneasiness she had caused him. Determined not to let her guess how much she interested him, he took her by the hand and gently pulled her out onto the front porch. "I thought I should kiss you under the porch light for the benefit of any neighbors who might be watching," he said.

His hand holding hers was already sending currents of excitement shooting through her. Her legs weakened at this announcement of his further intent. *You're behaving like a schoolgirl,* she chided herself. But as he released her hand and cupped her face, every fiber of her being was aware of him.

Reid didn't think he'd ever touched a woman who felt so soft. His fingers entwined in her hair, and he looked down into the deep brown depths of her eyes.

The blue of Reid's eyes reminded Celina of the sky on a hot summer afternoon. Her heart began to pound so hard she was afraid he might hear it.

Reid saw the flicker of uncertainty in her gaze, then it was overshadowed by the flare of passion. That she wasn't immune to him pleased him. Lowering his head, he kissed her lightly. She tasted sweeter than any woman had ever tasted to him.

Celina thought her body was going to ignite. Never in her life had anything caused her to feel such intense excitement.

The muscles in Reid's arms tensed as he fought to keep from tightening his embrace. He wanted to feel every curve of her molded to him. *Control yourself,* he ordered, shaken by the strength of his urge to carry her back inside and continue this kiss in private. Forcing himself to release her, he took a step back.

Celina's body rebelled at his desertion. Of their own volition, her legs started to move her toward him. She had to force herself to stop. *Now I know what it must feel like to be a moth drawn to a flame,* she thought, her blood still racing.

Reid saw his own desire mirrored in her eyes. "A week of courtship and another week to plan the wedding should suffice," he said, signing the words with sharp movements as he fought to keep from pulling her back into his arms.

"Yes," she agreed in a voice barely above a whisper.

"I'll be by at six again tomorrow," he said, then turning away from her, walked toward his car. To himself he added, "And I'll think of something public to do." He didn't like being this attracted to a woman. These feelings won't last, he assured himself. As proof, he recalled his parents and their marriages. Obviously this kind of strong physical attraction was what they thought of as love. But he knew better. It was a fire that would quickly burn itself out.

Celina leaned against the wall of her house as she watched him drive away. She'd heard about this kind of reaction to a man. But she'd been sure the stories were exaggerations. Now she knew they weren't. Her heart was still pounding wildly and the flame he had ignited still burned hot. *At least the part of our marriage where he sires the children shouldn't be any problem for me,* she told herself.

Chapter Five

"I've had three phone calls already this morning from people wanting to know about you and Dr. Prescott," Adelle informed Celina the next morning as they sat at Celina's kitchen table waiting for the percolator to finish brewing. Adelle had been on her niece's doorstep bright and early. "One woman has had her eye on Reid Prescott since he came to town. She wasn't at all happy about hearing that you and the doctor were spending time together. She wanted me to tell her that your relationship with the good doctor is strictly business, that he's consulting with you about your healing ability. The other two, however, think it's a perfect match—the healer and the doctor."

Mentally Celina groaned. Considering what a sore spot her reputation as a healer was with him, Reid would be furious when he heard this. He might even call off the wedding.

Adelle regarded her niece levelly. "Is Dr. Prescott one of the options you told me you were pursuing?"

"Yes," Celina replied, wondering if he would still be an option by noon.

A sternness crossed Adelle's features. "I do hope you intend to marry him, not just seduce him. Because his reputation would be marred as much as yours."

The thought of herself as a temptress caused Celina to smile. The thought of her seducing Reid Prescott was even more humorous. If he hadn't been desperate to find a wife and she hadn't needed a husband and Doc hadn't suggested that the two of them get together, she doubted he ever would have thought of her as anything other than a meddling nuisance. "I promise you, I will not have his child unless I marry him first," she assured her aunt.

Adelle breathed a noticeable sigh of relief.

The sudden blinking of the lights told Celina she had more company.

'I'll wager five dollars that's your grandmothers,' Adelle signed with authority.

"I never take sucker bets," Celina replied, certain Adelle was right.

"We just let ourselves in," Edna Warley said as she entered the kitchen at that moment, followed by Gale Tupper. Coming to an abrupt halt, she faced her granddaughter and demanded, "We want to know if you're seeing Dr. Prescott professionally or socially."

"Socially," Celina replied, and saw looks of relief on both their faces.

"I hope this means you're reconsidering being a single parent," Gale signed.

Celina nodded. "It does." And, now was as good a time as any to prepare them for a quick engagement announcement. "In fact, I was just going to ask Adelle to take a look at my mother's wedding gown and see if it needs any altering."

Shock replaced the relief on the faces of all three women. "Are you sure you aren't moving a bit too fast?" Edna questioned. Then realizing she had only spoken, she repeated this again in sign language.

"I caught what you said the first time," Celina said with an edge of impatience. She knew they loved her and wanted only the best for her. And she knew that the reason for at least some of her impatience was that she herself wasn't all that certain this marriage was for the best. Nevertheless it was the most acceptable solution. Turning to Grandma Tupper, she said in gentler tones, "You and Grandpa knew right away that you belonged together."

"Your grandfather did," Gale corrected. "It took me a week."

Still looking skeptical, Edna Warley said, "Dr. Prescott has always struck me as the kind of man who would bide his time before making a decision."

Celina gave what she hoped was a playful shrug. "It's probably going to take him a week or so before he's ready to announce our engagement, but I'm pretty sure he feels the same way I do." Seeing the three women exchange worried glances, Celina felt guilty for causing more anxiety. "Don't worry," she added quickly. "I won't be shattered if my expectations don't come true."

"You've always been a very realistic girl. I'm sure you'll handle whatever happens well," Gale Tupper said, the uneasiness on her face causing Celina to believe she was saying this as much for herself as for Celina.

"Expectations can sometimes lead to disappointment," Edna warned, her signing threatening to falter as if she didn't want to issue this warning but felt she must.

"I will be just fine," Celina assured them. "No matter what happens."

"Or what doesn't happen," she said aloud to herself that evening as she watched Reid coming up the walk. There was a stiffness in his carriage and a grim set to his jaw.

"It seems that by courting you, I've given validity to your healing abilities," he said, anger clearly evident in his expression and the sharpness of his hand gestures. "I suppose, in the eyes of the residents of Smytheshire, that my marrying you will be the same as handing you a medical diploma. I'll probably have to hang out a new shingle that reads, 'Dr. Reid Prescott, M.D., and Celina, Healer.' "

"Does this mean you've decided to call off our arrangement?" she asked.

Drawing in a terse breath, Reid regarded her in silence for a long moment. That thought had been the subject of a mental battle he'd been having with himself all day. His gaze raked her. She looked even more appealing than he remembered. Besides, he needed a wife. "No," he replied. "The damage is done. At least living with you, I can keep an eye on you."

Celina glared at him. "There is no need for you to feel you have to keep an eye on me."

Reid found himself wanting to do a whole lot more than just keep an eye on her. He wanted to pull her into his arms and kiss her. *I'm thinking like a teenager in lust,* he growled at himself. Well, marriage was sure to cure that quickly. Provided she was still willing to marry him, he qualified, seeing the anger sparking in her eyes. "I apologize," he said, signing in large gestures as he spoke. In more modified movements, he added, "It's been a difficult day. I never realized how many people were interested in my marital status."

As the anger left his expression, Celina saw the lines of tiredness on his face. She felt a stirring of sympathy, then told herself he didn't deserve it. Still, she could understand his loss of temper. She'd had more patrons in the library today than she usually had in a month. Some hadn't used their library card in years. All had managed to bring up Reid's name and mention they'd heard she was seeing him. By the end of the day she'd been ready to scream. "I'm used to everyone knowing everyone else's business," she said, "but even when a person is used to having their privacy pried into, it can be unnerving."

"Thanks for understanding," he said, finding it hard to believe she hadn't thrown him out. Then he reminded himself that she wanted a baby as much as he wanted his medical practice.

He was looking more exhausted by the moment and Celina had a sudden urge to pamper him. *He doesn't even really want to be here,* she admonished herself. Still, she found herself saying, "I'll fix us something to eat here. I think we've both made enough public appearances for one day."

Reid couldn't argue with that. Just the thought of facing a roomful of quizzical stares made him cringe.

"I hate to impose. We could get some takeout from the café," he offered.

"It's not an imposition," she replied, shaken by how much she honestly wanted to take care of him. Her humor surfacing to cover the uneasiness this realization caused, she added, "Besides, people will think you've definitely acted rashly if we get engaged before you've tasted my cooking."

Grateful she was willing to lighten the atmosphere, Reid grinned. "What happens if I don't like your cooking?"

"Then you learn to cook," she tossed back as she started toward the kitchen.

"You have one heck of a saucy walk, lady," he murmured to her back. "It could make a man forget all about your cooking."

A tingle ran through Celina. It was as if she could actually feel him watching her. Glancing over her shoulder, she saw a heated gleam in his eyes that sent a rush of warmth through her. She caught the movement of his lips. "Did you say something?" she asked.

"Just thinking aloud."

The urge to ask him what he had been thinking about was strong, but shyness held her back. She'd never been very good at flirting or bantering. Besides, he could have been thinking about some other woman she just happened to remind him of, she cautioned herself. And that was something she didn't want to know. Giving a shrug as if to say that his thoughts were his own business and didn't interest her, she continued into the kitchen.

Who he thinks about when he's with me doesn't matter. He is simply a necessary nuisance to achieve my goal of motherhood, she told herself as she opened the freezer and took out three individually wrapped chicken breasts.

But later that evening she had to admit that "nuisance" wasn't really a fair description.

He'd come into the kitchen shortly after she'd begun fixing their meal and insisted on helping. He'd been skeptical when he'd discovered she was starting with frozen chicken.

"I'll thaw your piece out before I serve it to you," she'd quipped.

He'd grinned self-consciously. "Guess I should leave the cooking to the cook," he'd said and busied himself with setting the table.

She'd liked his grin. It had an impish quality she never would have thought the cynical Dr. Prescott possessed. She also liked the fact that he hadn't argued with her. Men who always knew how to do everything grated on her nerves. At least this was a good start, she'd told herself.

During the meal, he'd paused periodically to make polite small talk and compliment her. Still, in spite of her efforts to relax, she'd felt strained. When she looked at him, her mind flashed back to the feel of his lips on hers, and then she would find herself wondering about what their wedding night would be like. By the time they'd finished the meal, her nerves were on a brittle edge. She adamantly refused his offer to help clear the table and wash the dishes. She insisted that he looked exhausted and sent him into the living room to read the paper and rest.

"I've got to learn to relax around him," she'd ordered herself as she'd put the last of the leftovers away and began scraping the dishes and putting them into the dishwasher. The frown on her face deepened. She wasn't going to accomplish that hiding out in her kitchen. Leaving the rest of the dishes for later, she'd headed for the living room.

There she'd found Reid seated on the couch with the paper in his hand, sound asleep. He was so exhausted that when she'd removed his shoes and gently suggested he lie down, he'd obeyed without even fully waking up.

This was good, she'd told herself. She could sit in here with him while he slept and get used to having him around.

That had been nearly two hours ago. She'd seated herself in the chair opposite the couch and tried to concentrate on the newspaper. But her gaze had kept shifting to him. Finally she'd given up on the paper and was now simply watching him sleep. What was curious was that he looked as if he belonged exactly where he was. In spite of the fact it was a hot summer night, the urge to join him, to snuggle up next to him, crept over her. Again she recalled his kiss, and the embers of desire ignited within her.

No, "nuisance" was definitely not a fair description. When she'd been a teenager, she'd had a couple of crushes. But it had been a long time since any man had been able to inspire desire. The truth was she'd begun to worry that she'd somehow become frigid. But Reid Prescott had rid her of this fear. The thought of their wedding night again entered her mind. Excitement mingled with a new fear. What if he wasn't a considerate lover? What if he treated their lovemaking as a clinical exercise? As long as the result is a child, how he does it doesn't matter, she assured herself.

She glanced at the clock. It was almost ten. Like the needle on a compass being drawn to the magnetic north, her gaze shifted back to him. He's not that good-looking, she chided herself, troubled by how fully he claimed her attention.

Giving herself a shake, she rose and approached the couch. Gently she touched him on the shoulder. The contact caused a current of excitement to race up her arm.

Reid awoke with a start. To his surprise he felt refreshed. "Sorry, I seem to have dozed off," he apologized through a yawn. Then, to make sure he was understood, he quickly signed his words.

"You obviously needed the rest," she replied, taking a step back to put distance between them. In spite of the fact that she was relieved to know she wasn't frigid, the strength of her reaction to him still unnerved her.

He glanced at the clock. Embarrassment spread over his face. "I really am sorry. It seems I've been asleep a long time."

Celina gave a shrug. "We had a quiet evening at home similar to what a lot of married couples have and survived it," she said. "But now I think you should be leaving."

Reid nodded and pushed himself to his feet. "Thanks for dinner," he signed. As he headed toward the front door, he caught her hand and drew her along with him. He told himself that the good-night kiss was necessary for the neighbors' sake. Then he laughed at himself. He *wanted* to kiss her.

On the porch, he drew her into his arms. She tasted as sweet as she had the night before. As her body swayed against his, a close to overwhelming impatience to claim her fully swept through him. Disturbed by the strength of his attraction, he forced himself to release her and leave.

What was even more unsettling, he admitted as he climbed into his car, was how rested he felt. Memories of his youth flooded over him. He'd lived in a great many homes, but he couldn't remember ever living in one as comfortable as hers. A wry smile tilted one corner of his mouth. "I never lived in a home where I didn't feel like I had to prove I was useful enough to earn my place there," he muttered. He'd expected to experience at least a hint of that in her home but he hadn't. "Because I already know how I'm supposed to earn my place and I know we will both benefit from this arrangement." He drew a relieved breath. This marriage was going to work out just fine. And he didn't have to worry about the complications love always seemed to cause in a relationship.

Celina watched him drive away, then went back inside and finished putting the dishes in the dishwasher. But even as she worked, the image of him asleep on the couch filled her mind. After starting the dishwasher, she wandered back into the living room and sank down into the chair she'd occupied earlier.

Staring at the now empty couch, she wondered if she would have had the nerve to join him there even if they were married. Or if she'd even want to, she added, anxiety about their wedding night returning.

Her hand moved to her lips, and the memory of his kiss brought a rush of heated excitement. If his lovemaking was half as enjoyable as his kiss, she'd be satisfied.

Chapter Six

Well, today is the day all my questions will be answered, Celina thought as a fresh wave of panic swept through her. It was approximately two weeks since the evening Reid napped on her couch. They'd announced their engagement a few days after that and set the wedding date for the following Wednesday.

On Monday of this week, the telephone people had come. Until now, the only phone she had in the house was the one in the living room with the TDD attached. Her grandparents and Aunt Adelle had similar Telecommunication Devices for the Deaf on their phones. The instrument, which looked like a small typewriter and had, above the keyboard, a one-line screen on which the message being typed between machines appeared, allowed her to communicate with these family members over the phone lines. Reid, however, had wanted another phone installed in the bedroom so that he could easily receive night calls. He'd had a wall phone installed in the kitchen, as well.

Yesterday, he'd moved his belongings into her home. This morning when she awoke, she'd stood looking at his clothing hanging in the closet in her bedroom. Apprehension had mingled with nervous expectation.

By the time her grandmothers and Aunt Adelle arrived to help her dress for the wedding, she was struggling to keep her hands from shaking. But now, finally, she was dressed, and they were all gathered in the hall ready to leave for the church.

Adelle's gaze raked Celina, making one last inventory. "We want to do this right," she said. "We don't want to forget anything important."

"I think we've thought of everything," Edna Warley said, her gaze traveling searchingly over Celina as well. "Your mother's wedding dress is the 'something old.' The hankie Gale embroidered with your wedding date and yours and Reid's names on it is the 'something new.' The pearl earrings Adelle loaned you, the 'something borrowed' and the blue lace on your garter the 'something blue.'"

"The penny! We forgot the penny for luck in her shoe!" Gale Tupper exclaimed.

"I'm sure I have one," Adelle said, rummaging in her purse.

A sudden thought struck Celina. The penny she'd found in her garden the day Reid Prescott had first come to her home was on the sill of the window over her kitchen sink. So many things had happened the day she'd found it she'd forgotten she'd put the dirty coin in her pocket. The next Saturday, she'd discovered it in the bottom of her washing machine. She'd taken it out and put it in her pocket again. But this time she'd remembered it was there while she was fixing her lunch. Afraid she'd forget about it again, she'd taken it out of her pocket and put it on the window-sill. The sunlight had glinted on it and she'd grinned. Her buried treasure, she'd mused again and left it there.

"I have a penny," she said and, before anyone could respond, she went quickly into the kitchen. "You were there when Reid Prescott first came into my life," she murmured quietly to the copper coin. "He's going to stay for a short while and you might as well come along for the ride. I know that traditionally the luck you're supposed to bring to the marriage focuses on prosperity—the bride shall have luxuries and never want for material things. In this case, though, I'm not interested in monetary wealth. The prosperity I'm counting on you bringing me is a child." She slipped the penny into her shoe. Not wanting to be selfish, she added quickly, "However, for Reid's sake, you could see that he gets his contract. That way we both will prosper, each in our own way."

Celina drew a breath of relief. It was now late afternoon, and the ceremony was over. The photographer had finished snapping pictures and she, Reid and the rest of the wedding party were on their way to join the guests for the reception. It was taking place in the Fellowship Hall, attached to the church, and the ladies' auxiliary was preparing the dinner. All in all, other than the speed with which the wedding had been planned, the event was totally in keeping with the traditions of their little town. *Except, of course, for the reasons we're getting married,* Celina amended.

"I hope you don't mind if I shed another tear or two now that the pictures have been taken," Sheree Komanski, Reid's mother, said, already beginning to weep daintily. "This has just been so beautiful."

Celina forced a smile. Reid had told her that his mother had a tendency to be dramatic. "Tendency," Celina had learned very quickly, was an understatement.

Reid's mother was beautiful. She was small-boned, with a tall, slender figure. Her tinted blond hair was perfectly coiffed and her nails and makeup were as professional as a model's. When she'd arrived yesterday, she'd been dressed in black leather pants that looked as if she'd been poured into them, a fitted blouse opened to her bra line, a black leather vest and four-inch black heels. The rest of her wardrobe had proved to be just as sexy. Celina had to admit that at fifty-two, Sheree Komanski looked more like thirty. And behaved, she thought, more like sixteen—an immature sixteen.

Celina's mind flashed back to yesterday evening. Reid had been called out on an emergency and hadn't been at the church when his mother had arrived for the wedding rehearsal. Adelle, however, had been present. At first, Sheree had leaned close to Celina and pronounced each word with exaggerated lip movements as she explained that she and her current husband, Bill, had nearly missed the rehearsal entirely. "Actually we nearly missed Smytheshire. Bill—" she'd paused to give the quiet, short, plumpish, fifty-five-year-old man at her side a little tap on the shoulder "—missed the turnoff from the main road. We'd crossed the border into Vermont and were headed for Canada before he'd listen to me and turn around," she'd proclaimed. Then, noticing Adelle standing near her shoulder signing her words to Celina, she'd grinned broadly and placed her arm around Adelle's shoulders. "I'm claiming you as my official interpreter," she'd informed Adelle. Wrapping her other arm around Celina's shoulders, she'd added, "We shall be inseparable. I want to get to know my soon-to-be daughter-in-law."

And she had been true to her word, in a manner of speaking. Sheree had demanded the majority of Celina's time before and after the rehearsal. She had, however, devoted their conversation to her own marriages. "I'm such a passionate person," she'd said with an exaggerated sigh as she finished telling about how she'd met and married Bill. "I just can't seem to control my emotions. They just explode and carry me with them."

Celina had caught the cynical glimmer in Adelle's eyes while Bill had sat beaming proudly at the description of himself as an ardent Don Juan with the ability to sweep women off their feet with the mere flicker of a eye.

Unable to completely control her curiosity, several times Celina had tried to turn the conversation toward Reid. When Reid's father had called a couple of days ago to say he wouldn't be able to make it to the ceremony, she'd been disappointed. Reid never talked about his past. The morning after they'd announced their engagement and her grandmothers had begun asking questions about Reid's family, she'd realized just how little she knew about her future husband. Normally she prided herself on not prying into the lives of other. But, she reasoned, this was different. It was only natural for a woman to want to know something about her husband's childhood. But she wasn't any more successful at learning anything about him from Sheree than she had been from Reid himself. Each time Celina guided the conversation toward Reid, his mother would say something to the effect that he was always much too quiet and serious, then launch into an antic of hers that showed how different she was from her son.

A couple of times during the evening, Reid had tried to interrupt and free Celina from his mother, but Sheree had been persistent. Finally Celina had signed to him that she didn't mind and he'd given up his efforts.

This morning, as Adelle, Grandma Tupper and Grandma Warley had sat around Celina's kitchen table drinking coffee and exchanging women talk before the time arrived to prepare for the ceremony, Adelle had prophesied that Sheree would attempt to be the center of attention at the wedding.

"If I hear once more about how 'passionate' she is, I think I'll throw up," Edna Warley had said, with a shake of her head.

"I swear that woman doesn't know the difference between love and lust," Gale Tupper had replied sternly.

Celina hadn't said anything, but now she could easily understand why Reid was so cynical about marriage.

And Adelle had been right about Sheree's attempting to be the center of attention. The woman had wept openly during the ceremony. In the reception line afterward, she'd apologized to each guest for her smeared makeup, explaining that she couldn't stop crying, because the ceremony had been so beautiful.

Then she'd added that it reminded her so much of her own last wedding, at which point she'd launched into a description of her nuptials with Bill. Finally she'd delayed the picture-taking by another twenty minutes so that she could redo her makeup.

But now the picture-taking was finished and the wedding party was on its way to Fellowship Hall. Sheree was on Celina's right talking animatedly while Adelle was next to Sheree continuing to sign the woman's words. Suddenly Adelle's face quirked into a grimace and she signed, "She's talking about her passionate nature again. I swear I'm ready to douse her with a garden hose."

Celina started to give her aunt a knowing smile when Adelle's cheeks reddened. Glancing over her left shoulder, Celina saw the self-conscious expression on Reid's face and knew he'd seen what Adelle had signed to her.

Adelle quickly began signing exactly what Sheree was saying but Celina barely caught any it. Until that moment Reid had exhibited, for the most part, an indifference toward his mother's behavior. Once in a while, he'd seemed to be wryly amused. Now Celina realized that beneath the surface, he was embarrassed. It occurred to her that he could use a friend. Slipping her hand into his, she gave it a squeeze.

Reid felt the pressure of Celina's hand. Sheree had been in top form since she'd arrived in Smytheshire. Most women, he guessed, would have been ready to douse his mother with a garden hose and demand an immediate annulment to the marriage. But Celina was offering him her support. *She must want that child really badly,* he told himself. Still, he gave her a grateful smile.

Celina's heart lurched at the sight of his crooked grin. Sheree was forgotten as she once again thought about being alone with Reid and nervousness battled with anticipation. Then they entered the hall and she was swept up into the midst of her relatives and friends. During the next few hours, she ate, visited, cut the wedding cake and visited some more.

Finally Adelle tapped her on the shoulder. "It's time for you to throw your bouquet and for Reid to throw the garter, and then the two of you leave," she signed.

Celina's entire body stiffened. She considered insisting on staying a while longer, then she caught a glance of Sheree with her grandmothers. Both of the elderly women looked as if their patience was at the breaking point. Nodding her consent, she watched as Adelle clanged on a glass to get everyone's attention for the final festivities.

Celina's smile felt plastic as she tossed the bouquet. But when Reid began removing the garter, his fingers brushed against her calf and the heat his touch could so easily produce burst into flame. *As long as I don't have an attack of nerves and jump, screaming hysterically, from the bed, everything should be fine,* she told herself.

She told herself that again as she and Reid drove to her house. Nevertheless, every muscle in her body tensed. She was used to living in a world of silence but the stillness between her and Reid at this moment seemed much more intense than anything she had ever experienced.

"I thought the wedding went well," she said, making an attempt at small talk.

"Yes," he replied, nodding.

Celina frowned at herself. He needed to remain facing the road and keep his hands on the wheel. That limited his side of the conversation to "yes" or "no." So much for small talk to ease her nerves, she mused.

At least they didn't have far to go, she thought with relief as he pulled into her driveway. Being careful not to harm her mother's wedding gown, she climbed out of the car before Reid could come around and assist her and headed toward the back door. A hand suddenly closed around her arm, and she was brought to an abrupt halt.

"Not so fast," Reid said. Releasing her so that he could sign his words, he continued, "This may not be a marriage for all the traditional reasons, but this is a traditional town we live in and you have traditional neighbors."

In the next instant, Celina found herself being lifted into his arms and carried toward the front porch. His after-shave filled her senses. In spite of the layers of clothing between them, she felt the heat of his body permeating hers. Her heart began to pound.

When they reached the door, he set her on her feet only long enough to unlock it. Then, lifting her again, he carried her over the threshold and into the house.

Her breath threatened to lock in her lungs as she waited for him to continue with her up the stairs to the bedroom they would share. But instead, she discovered herself again being set down on her feet.

Reid drew a terse breath and took a step back. He'd wanted to continue with her up to their bed. But he'd promised himself, Doc and her two grandfathers that he would behave with patience and control. "I can understand why people leave town on their honeymoon," he said, feeling the need to say something to keep his mind off undressing her right there in the hall. "The last week has been hectic. I could use a vacation. I'm sorry we couldn't arrange to get away for a few days." A rush of anger flowed through him as apology etched itself into his features. "And I'm sorry about my mother's behavior. I shouldn't have invited her. But she did promise to remember this was your day and not hers."

Celina had been feeling deserted. But seeing his discomfort, she felt a surge of sympathy for him. "It's all right. She's your mother. She should have been here. I'm just sorry your father couldn't make it," she added honestly. She'd reminded herself a hundred times during the past few days that they'd agreed to an arrangement that was more like a business deal. But now that she'd met Reid's mother, she couldn't stop herself from being even more curious about his father.

Reid gave an indifferent shrug. "He's a little hard to pin down. He likes jobs that keep him on the move. Guess that's one of the reasons he can never keep a wife. He has a tendency to forget he has a home."

The image of a young blond-haired boy sitting alone on the stairs in an empty house suddenly filled Celina's mind. "You must have had a very lonely childhood," she said gently.

An iciness flowed through him. He hadn't asked for, nor did he want, her sympathy. "I had an independent childhood," he corrected. "It taught me to stand on my own, to rely on myself and no one else."

Celina saw the cold pride in his eyes. "And never let anyone get too close to your heart," she signed.

"It's a comfortable way to live my personal life," he replied, noting that he was very satisfied with his chosen path. "I've got enough stress in my professional life. I'll happily leave the emotional 'roller coaster of love,' as my mother likes to refer to her wavering affections, to others."

The way he signed "roller coaster of love" showed his distaste. And the resolute set of his jaw left no doubt in her mind that he would allow no one to touch his heart. "A determinedly dispassionate man," she observed.

Reid wished he was a little more dispassionate where she was concerned. When they'd left the church, he'd been having some very lusty thoughts about her. In the past few moments his ardor had cooled slightly. But as his gaze traveled over her, his attention was drawn to the soft rise and fall of her lace-covered breasts, and the urge to sweep her up in his arms again and carry her upstairs grew strong. He couldn't remember ever wanting a woman so badly. He grinned crookedly at the strength of his hunger. "I am not without my desires," he said.

Celina saw the blue of his eyes deepen and a heat raced through her. "Lucky for me," she replied.

"You are a very tempting sight," he signed, wondering how he was going to force himself to move slowly.

"You look pretty good yourself," she replied, then in her nervousness added, "Of course, I've never seen you without your clothes on." Her cheeks flushed scarlet when she realized what she'd said.

Reid's grin broadened. She looked delectable when she was disconcerted, he thought. "Is that an invitation?"

He signed as he spoke, and watching his hands, she couldn't stop thinking about how they would feel on her body. A part of her was anxious to discover if they were as warm as his lips, while another part was growing more nervous by the moment. "I suppose it was," she said, attempting to sound saucy. After all, she reasoned, she had married him to have a child.

Reid wanted to believe her. But he was used to looking for small nuances in patients that would tell him if they weren't being completely honest, and he saw the hesitation in her eyes. *Or maybe I'm just a little more nervous about this than I'm willing to admit,* he thought. He'd told himself earlier that she was merely interested in his aiding her in producing a child. But now he found himself wanting her to enjoy his aid. *My ego must be bigger than I thought,* he scoffed at himself. A sudden inspiration struck him. "How about a few hands of strip poker?" he suggested.

Celina blinked. He wanted to play cards?

Maybe that wasn't so inspired, he thought, watching the shocked expression on her face.

But as her initial surprise wore off, it occurred to Celina that discarding their clothing slowly would give her time to become more relaxed in his presence. "Sounds like a fun idea," she said.

A picture of her seated across from him in her lacy underthings suddenly filled his mind. The game might be fun, but it was definitely going to be trying on his patience, he decided as she went into the living room and got a deck of cards.

"I suppose the bedroom would be the best place for this little game," she said, rejoining him.

Reid nodded. "After you," he signed, ending with a flourish as he gestured toward the stairs and bowed from the waist.

Preceding him up the stairs, Celina felt her legs weakening. *Relax,* she ordered herself. Entering the bedroom, she marched up to the bed and seated herself cross-legged on it with her wedding gown spread out around her.

As Reid seated himself, she took the cards out of their box and shuffled them. "Is five-card stud all right with you?" she asked.

He nodded and she began to deal.

He won the first hand and she discarded her veil.

She won the second and he discarded his suit jacket.

Next came his shoes.

"This is fun," she admitted, as she lost the next hand and pulled out a hairpin.

"Hairpins all come out at once," he stipulated, reaching over and helping her free her hair from the stylish curls Gabrielle Rutland had spent two hours that morning arranging. As the auburn tresses cascaded over her shoulders, he leaned forward and kissed her lightly. Then he forced himself to straighten away from her and pick up the deck of cards.

This was more difficult than he'd thought it would be, he admitted. She was still fully clothed and he was having a hard time keeping his hands off of her.

The heat of his lips lingered tantalizingly on Celina's while the scent of his after-shave created havoc with her senses. A sudden burst of impatience swept through her. When he lost the next hand and removed his tie, her impatience grew.

"Why don't we just cut the deck this time. High card wins," she suggested.

Reid saw the fire in her eyes and smiled. "In case of a tie, we both remove something," he added.

Celina grinned her consent.

She lost the first cut and kicked off her shoes. Vaguely she noted that the penny rolled under the bed.

"The dress is next," Reid warned.

He'd managed to make his hand signs look absolutely lecherous, Celina thought, laughing lightly. But when she lost, her nerves once again became taut. Standing beside the bed, she tried to look nonchalant as she attempted to work the small buttons at the back of the neck loose. But she was all thumbs.

"Seems like you need a little help," he said. He knew he should stay away from her, but she was having so much trouble he had the sudden vision of the two of them being there till midnight before the dress was off.

Celina nodded.

Reid stood up and began to undo the buttons. When they were free, he slid the zipper down and the dress began to fall away. Unable to resist, he leaned forward and kissed the newly exposed skin of her shoulder. It was warm and tasted sweet.

Celina trembled from pure delight. Turning toward him, she said, "One good turn deserves another. The next time you lose, I'll unbutton your shirt."

Didn't she know how dangerous she was to a man's control? Reid thought, watching as her dress continued its downward slide, exposing her lacy underthings. His fantasized vision of her hadn't done her justice, he admitted, as he forced himself to step back and reseat himself on his side of the bed.

As she finished removing the dress and hung it in the closet, Celina was aware of his gaze. It almost seemed to warm her and she wished he'd kissed her other shoulder.

She returned to the bed and cut the cards. This time he lost. Leaning forward, she began working the buttons of his shirt. She shifted closer as the heat of his body teased her fingertips. When the last button was unfastened, she eased the shirt off him. He looked very sturdy, she thought approvingly. Unable to resist testing this theory, she ran her hands over his shoulders. The muscles tensed beneath her palms giving evidence of their power, and the fires that had been burning within her flamed hotter.

"You're making my moving slowly very difficult," Reid growled as she continued her exploration.

Delighting in the masculine feel of him, Celina had been concentrating on the texture of his hair-roughened chest. When she caught a glimpse of his lips moving, she stopped and looked up at him questioningly. "What did you say?"

"I said," he replied, this time signing as he spoke, "that you are testing my patience."

Celina saw her own desire reflected in the blue depths of his eyes. "I know that patience is a virtue," she said. "But there are times when it can be a nuisance."

Reid noted that this time her manner held no hint of hesitation. He leaned forward to kiss the pulse at her neck and felt its warm throbbing beneath his lips. Straightening, he picked up the deck of cards and bent them, then released them in an arcing shower that sent them flying out into the room. He turned back to her, and said, "I just won. I get to finish undressing you."

Celina laughed. "And as the loser, do I only get to watch you strip or do I get to undress you, too?"

Reid grinned. "It's your choice."

''I'll think about it while you work,'' she returned, forcing her expression into one of deep contemplation.

Celina Warley was a great deal more playful than he had thought she would be, Reid admitted, as he began his task. And very sexy, he added.

A fresh wave of nervousness swept through Celina as Reid worked. But the approval she saw in his eyes vanquished it. His fingers, as they brushed her, sent surges of pleasure rushing through her. There was also a sensation of power that radiated from his touch, enthralling and enticing her. Her blood raced and a feeling of well-being mingled with heated excitement. Her own patience gone, she reached for his belt and began unfastening it.

Giving up all pretext of moving slowly, Reid drew her into his arms for a hard, demanding kiss. Never had Celina felt the need to be so physically close to another person. Her fingers wove into his hair and she arched against him.

Reid growled with pleasure. Trailing kisses as he went, he finished removing her undergarments.

Celina smiled as she saw the passion in his eyes. Deftly she began removing his clothing. She'd thought she would be embarrassed or at least shy the first time she saw him unclothed. But she experienced neither. Interest mingled with delight.

Feeling as if her body needed his to be whole, Celina took his hand and pulled him toward the bed.

Knowing his limitations, Reid admitted he could not wait much longer. Accepting her unspoken invitation, he went without hesitation.

As they lay down, his touch became more intimate, and for one brief instant, Celina experienced a flutter of fear. Then he moved to claim her and all thoughts but those of him and pleasing him as much as he was pleasing her left her mind.

Celina was grinning softly the next morning as she gathered up the discarded clothing. Her wedding night had been even more enjoyable than she'd thought possible. A shaft of sunlight struck a glint of copper under the bed. "The lucky penny," she said, her grin broadening. Maybe she should leave it there. After all, she did want its luck to focus on the physical union in this marriage. On the other hand, the penny might get vacuumed up if she left it on the floor. Deciding on a compromise, she slipped it in between the mattress and the box spring.

Her gaze shifted to the bathroom. Reid was showering and she found herself picturing him soaking wet and unclothed. A heat stirred within her. Although the urge to join him was strong, she didn't want him to think she was wanton. But then, she reasoned, she was his wife and he had agreed to get her pregnant. Deciding the room could wait, she went in to join him in the shower.

Chapter Seven

Celina sat on her front porch enjoying the summer evening. It was Friday. She'd been married for two days. Even though she and Reid hadn't been able to leave town for a honeymoon, they'd both arranged to take Thursday off. A lazy smile played across her face as she recalled how exhilarating yesterday had been, beginning with their shower. Reid hadn't minded her joining him at all. Last night and this morning had also been extraordinarily enjoyable. Reid had proved to be a most ardent lover. Just thinking about him caused the fires of desire to ignite again.

A tap on her shoulder reminded her that Aunt Adelle was seated in the chair beside her. Looking toward her, she saw Adelle grin and sign, "Looks like married life agrees with you."

Celina nodded as she smiled back sheepishly. Almost as soon as she'd gotten home from work, Adelle had arrived to relay a message that Reid would be delayed. The Miller boy had taken a fall and needed some emergency care.

"Reid has a TDD on order for his office. It should be here sometime today or tomorrow," she said, flushing slightly as her aunt continued to regard her with amusement. "Then he can communicate with me by phone and you won't have to keep running over here to tell me when he'll be late."

"I really didn't mind relaying the message," Adelle assured her. Her smile broadened. "It's nice to see you so happy."

For one brief moment, Celina felt a pang of fear. She was happy. But there was no guarantee how long this would last. Reid could get bored with her. In fact, he probably would. And once he had the lease for the office and she was pregnant, he might feel no need to remain with her. She decided to cross that bridge when she came to it. For now, she would concentrate on the present. "I am enjoying myself," she replied.

Adelle laughed. "That's obvious."

Abruptly Adelle's attention shifted toward the street. Following her aunt's line of vision, Celina saw a red car cruising slowly toward them. She didn't recognize it. She glanced toward Adelle and saw her give a shrug. Apparently Adelle didn't recognize the car, either.

The driver parked in front of Celina's house and climbed out carrying a gift-wrapped package. She was a pretty brunette, medium in build, dressed in a loose-fitting blouse, summer-weight cotton slacks and sandals. As she passed through the gate and approached the porch, Celina saw a sprinkling of gray in the brown hair and realized the woman was older than she'd first thought. Probably in her late forties, she decided as the caller drew closer.

The woman waved and Celina saw her lips form the word "Hi," then, "I'm looking for Reid and Celina Prescott." The woman looked down at a sheet of paper she was holding in her free hand. Her lips moved, but she was now looking away and Celina couldn't see what she was saying. She glanced at her aunt.

"You do have the right address," Adelle was saying.

Celina rose. "I'm Celina," she said.

The woman smiled brightly as she mounted the porch steps. But there was a puzzled look in her eyes. "Reid's dad told me you were deaf."

"I can read lips," Celina replied. She nodded at Adelle. "This is my Aunt Adelle. If you speak at a moderate speed, she'll sign your words to make certain I don't miss anything you're saying."

The woman smiled at Adelle. "I figured they'd be gone on a honeymoon and I'd leave this package with one of the neighbors."

"We couldn't arrange our work schedules so that we could get away," Celina said, catching most of what the woman was saying without Adelle having to sign it.

The woman's gaze darted back to Celina. Curiosity mingled with kindness in her eyes. "I'm Joanna Lewis. I was Eric Prescott's, Reid's dad, second wife. People call me Jo." She extended her hand. "I'm pleased to meet you."

Interest burned strong in Celina as she accepted the handshake. More than ever, she found herself wanting to know more about Reid's past. *You're going to get hurt if you start caring too much about the man,* she warned herself for the hundredth time. Again she ordered herself to think of him merely as the man who would father her child. But this opportunity to learn more about him was too tantalizing to overlook. *Besides, because he's to be the father of my child, I should try to learn something about his past,* she decided. *In case our child asks someday, I'll have something to tell him or her.* "It's nice to meet you, too," she replied.

"Eric's never been good at doing family things. When he got Reid's message about getting married, he called and asked me to choose a wedding gift and see that Reid and you got it," she said, extending the package toward Celina. "He was kind of vague about what I should get, so I just used my own judgment. It's a waffle iron. I remember I made waffles for Reid when he came to stay with us, and he used to eat a ton."

"Thank you," Celina said accepting the gift. This was the first time anyone, including Reid, had told her what kind of food he'd liked as a child. She suddenly found herself picturing a little blond boy seated at a kitchen table with a plate of waffles in front of him and a big grin on his face.

"Eric also asked me to apologize for his not being able to make it to the wedding," Jo continued. "He had to be at some big auto race out West somewhere, I think. I can't remember just where. That man is always on the move. He's working as a mechanic for a pit crew on one of those expensive racing cars right now. Before that it was oil exploration on a rig in some sea somewhere. When we first met and got married, he was hooked up with a bunch of divers searching for sunken treasure off the coast of Florida. That didn't

pan out, so he went up to Alaska looking for gold."
She shook her head. "It got so that if I wanted to see
him, I had to go looking for him."

Celina remembered that Reid had said his father
wasn't home much. It didn't sound like the man ever
was. "That can be a strain on a marriage," she said.

Jo nodded. "It sure can. But I knew what kind of
man he was when I married him. Guess I thought I
could change him. Should have listened to my mother.
She used to say trying to change a man was like trying
to change your hair color. The roots always remain the
same and keep showing through."

Celina caught the look of affirmation in Adelle's
eyes as she finished signing this last statement. Jo,
meanwhile, paused to shake her head at her own stu
pidity.

"Anyway, once I accepted the fact that he would
always be a little boy at heart, we parted on good terms
and still keep in touch," Jo continued. Apology entered her expression. "He asked me to come to the
wedding, but I really can't stomach Sheree. Never met
a woman so wrapped up in herself."

It occurred to Celina that both of Reid's parents
were extremely self-centered. "It was nice of you to
bring the gift by," she said. "I hope this wasn't too far
out of your way."

Jo shrugged. "No. I live in Delaware now. But I've
been planning to go visit some friends in Vermont."
She grinned sheepishly. "Truth is, I was curious to see
how Reid had turned out."

"He's turned out very well," Adelle said with firm
conviction before Celina could even respond.

Jo smiled. "I'm glad to hear that. I've always felt a
little guilty. When his parents got divorced he was

barely five. His mom, of course, got custody. She immediately turned him over to his grandmother to raise. When he was ten, his grandmother died and there was Sheree with a kid on her hands. Well, she called Eric and told him she thought the boy needed his father. In the end, they agreed that he'd spend the nine months he was in school each year with her. But Eric got him for the summers. That was when Eric decided to marry me. Guess he felt he needed a home for the boy. And he did try to be around some during the months Reid was with us. But like I said, Eric wasn't the kind of man to be tied down. Anyway, the summer Reid was fifteen, I had pretty much decided that when the boy left, I was going to leave, too. I tried to make Reid's time with us as happy as possible. His dad was gone most of the time, but Reid and I did a lot together. I remember his coming into the kitchen a few days before he was scheduled to go back to his mom. He looked real nervous and I wondered what was wrong. Then he asked me if he could stay.''

A sadness shadowed Jo's eyes. ''I told him about my plans to leave his father. I liked the kid. I also figured that neither Sheree nor Eric would have really cared if he'd stayed with me. But I couldn't take on the responsibility. I was just getting ready to go out on my own again. Reid didn't say anything, he just nodded and went back up to his room. He left a couple of days later and I never saw him again.'' Her expression brightened. ''But Eric told me he'd become a doctor.''

''A very good one,'' Celina affirmed. She could understand the woman's reasons for not keeping the teenage boy. But she could also see how this rejection could have added more substance to Reid's cynical view of relationships.

Jo smiled. "He was always real bright."

It occurred to Celina that she had learned more about Reid in the past few minutes than in all the days she'd spent with him. And, she admitted, she still wanted to know more. "Reid's going to be getting home a little late," she said. "I've got a stew on the stove. There's plenty. I'd be pleased if you'd stay for dinner. That will give you a chance to visit with Reid." Rationalizing that this woman was the closest thing to family on Reid's father's side she was likely to meet, she added, "And you're welcome to stay the night."

"I've already taken a room at the Wainwright Inn," Jo replied. "But I'll be happy to stay for dinner."

As the three women went inside in search of something cool to drink, Celina realized she was a little nervous about what Reid's reaction would be to their dinner guest. He'd been so guarded about his past she wondered if he would see her invitation to Jo as an invasion of his privacy. But even if she wasn't interested in learning more about him, inviting Jo for dinner was only the polite thing to do, she reasoned. After all, the woman had come a long way to see him.

Adelle remained to continue signing so that Celina and Jo could converse without difficulty. And Adelle did exactly what Celina knew she would do. She began asking questions about Reid's childhood. *Well, at least I'm not the one prying,* Celina thought, trying not to feel so guilty about her own curiosity.

As Jo reminisced, a picture formed in Celina's mind of a child forced to become independent at a very young age. This image was strengthened when Jo talked about a camping trip she, Eric and Reid had taken in the Rockies. "Reid was only eleven then," Jo said, "but I don't think I've ever known a more self-sufficient child. We'd get up in the morning, and he'd have the fire going and the coffee brewing. Once, when we slept real late, he'd even gone down to the stream and caught a couple of fish for breakfast."

As Jo finished this story, Celina looked up to see Reid standing in the living-room doorway. She'd known he would be there. This realization stunned her. She hadn't "heard" him enter the house. It was as if she'd sensed his presence.

"I've always considered it an advantage to have learned early to stand on my own two feet," he said, letting Adelle and Jo know of his presence.

Celina saw the pride in his eyes as he signed his words with sharp, firm movements. He had learned more than just to stand on his own two feet, she thought. He'd learned to stand alone.

"Your father asked me to come by and bring a gift," Jo said, rising.

Celina only caught the first couple of words before the woman turned away from her. Quickly she glanced toward her aunt, who began signing the exchange between Reid and Jo. Their words were friendly, she noted. For verification of this, she periodically glanced at Reid. His expression was always polite and, every once in a while, he smiled. She breathed a sigh of relief, glad that he was not angry with her.

Celina insisted that Adelle also stay for dinner. With her aunt there, Reid and Jo could carry on a conversation without Reid constantly having to pause to interpret. But as Adelle tried to eat and keep up with signing the exchanges between Reid and Jo, Celina began to feel guilty. There was very little time for

Adelle to get her food from her plate to her mouth. Finally she signed to Adelle to stop signing and eat. But Adelle quickly flashed back that she was on a diet, anyway, and continued relaying what was being said.

As the meal progressed, Celina realized that she now knew more about Jo than she did about Reid. Most of the exchange between Reid and Jo was focused either on Jo and what she was doing with her life, or on Reid's adult life as a student and then as a doctor. Whenever Jo started to talk about his childhood, Reid would politely but firmly change the direction of the conversation.

When they were finished eating, Adelle helped Celina clean up the dishes while Reid and Jo went out to the front porch for some private talk. Celina told herself she shouldn't be interested. After all, she and Reid had more of a business arrangement than a marriage. Still, she couldn't help wondering what was being discussed. *You're thinking about him too much,* she admonished herself, and forced herself to concentrate on the dishes.

"Thanks for the lovely dinner," Jo said, rising from the rocking chair as Celina and Adelle joined her and Reid on the porch. "I hate to eat and run, but I'm exhausted from my long drive, and I want to get an early start tomorrow."

There was no evidence in the woman's expression to suggest that whatever she and Reid had been talking about was causing her to want to rush off, Celina noted as Reid rose and signed Jo's words. And she did look tired.

Jo shook her head and her smile became self-deprecating as she turned back toward Reid. "I can't believe I came here to find out how you were doing and ended up talking about myself almost the whole time."

As Adelle finished signing to Celina what Jo had said, Celina turned and studied Reid. Obviously he had continued his habit of avoiding talking about himself. A tap on her shoulder jerked her attention back to Adelle.

"I should be going, too," her aunt said.

Standing beside Reid on the porch waving goodbye to the two women, Celina covertly studied the man she'd married. Until this afternoon, she'd refused to admit to herself just how much she wanted to know more about him. A regret that she hadn't gotten to meet his father jabbed at her. "It's a shame your father couldn't come himself," she said, then flushed when she realized she'd spoken this thought aloud.

He glanced down at her. "You'd probably like him," he said, his expression emotionless as if he was relating an opinion about an acquaintance toward whom he felt only indifference. "He's got a real knack for charming women. I don't know of any other man who is still on such good terms with his ex-wives. He's entertaining, too, and can tell a good story."

It was obvious Reid did not feel close to his father. Celina also had to admit that although he'd been politely friendly toward Jo, she hadn't sensed any closeness between them, either. But at one time he must have felt something, at least for his stepmother, she reasoned, recalling what Jo had said about Reid's wishing to stay with her and his father. While telling herself that to persist would be prying, she couldn't stop herself from saying, "Jo seems like a real nice person."

"I owe her a great deal," he replied. "She taught me never to try to find security through others. It was a lesson worth learning. Through the years, I've found that most people have their own personal agendas. They allow others to share their lives only as long as those others fit into their plans or needs."

She frowned at his cynicism. "All people aren't as cold and selfish as you paint them. Sure there are some, but not everyone is that way."

He smiled humorlessly. "Perhaps you're right," he conceded. "The trick is being able to tell which ones are and which ones aren't. I choose not to bother."

She watched as he turned away from her and went inside. Clearly he was determined never to allow anyone to gain an emotional hold over him.

The urge was strong to go after him and try to convince him that taking a chance and letting others get near him was worth the risk. She went inside and found him sitting in the living room reading a medical journal that had arrived that day. His jaw was set in its usual resolute line. Coming to a halt in the doorway, she scowled at herself. *I would be smart to heed Jo's mother's advice about the futility of trying to change a man,* she told herself. *Especially when that man is Reid Prescott.* If ever she'd seen a person determined to live life on his own terms, it was him.

Just remember the bargain you've struck with him, she ordered herself. *Don't even allow yourself to think this marriage could become any more than what was agreed.* Turning away, she went upstairs.

Reid sat staring at the pages of the magazine in front of him. He'd heard Celina come in, pause at the door, then go upstairs. He guessed she wasn't pleased with his view of humanity but he had no wish to discuss it further.

When he'd walked in tonight and discovered Jo here, at first, he hadn't been pleased. The sight of her brought back an unpleasant memory. That day he'd asked her if he could remain with her had been the only time he'd ever asked anyone to allow him to stay. It was also the last. He'd sworn that he would never place himself in so vulnerable a position again.

He had, however, in the short time he'd been associated with Celina, grown uncomfortably used to her company. Today, while he was at the office, he'd even found himself thinking about her smile and about sitting quietly with her on the porch in the evenings. Having Jo come to visit had reminded him of how dangerous it could be to begin to rely on another person's continuing companionship. He drew a terse breath. He was glad she'd visited.

Chapter Eight

Two and a half weeks after she'd married Reid, Celina sat staring into her coffee. It was early morning and her new husband was still upstairs asleep. Saturdays were the only days Reid could sleep in, and he enjoyed staying in bed until ten or so. She, on the other hand, was a naturally early riser. But when she'd woken this morning, she hadn't immediately gotten up. Instead, she'd lain in bed watching him sleep.

She'd wanted to move closer to him, to snuggle into his arms. But this was not a good time of the month for physical intimacy. And physical intimacy was the only reason for her to seek Reid's attention in bed, she'd reminded herself. Simply enjoying lying close beside him would be asking for grave disappointment in the future. Determined to listen to her voice of sanity, she'd gotten out of bed, dressed and gone downstairs.

Her gaze shifted to her wedding ring. It was important to remain emotionally detached from the man upstairs, she knew.

A tap on her shoulder caused her to gasp and jerk around. Reid was standing there, barefoot, shirtless, wearing only a pair of jeans. His hair was mussed and he was unshaven. The memory of how delicious his whiskers felt against her skin caused a rush of heated excitement.

"Are you ill?" he asked, regarding her with the coolly analytical expression of a doctor addressing a patient.

"I'm just not used to lying in bed," she replied in a neutral tone. "And since we couldn't work on my pregnancy, I decided to get up."

Reid nodded understandingly. Admittedly, he conceded, he'd been slightly annoyed to awake alone. But he approved of her practical attitude. Now that he'd assured himself she was fine, he considered going back to bed, but the thought didn't appeal to him. Instead, he was filled with an odd restlessness. "Since we can't work on your part of our bargain, how about if we work on mine?" he suggested. "We could get dressed, have breakfast and then go for an early-morning stroll through town."

"So that you'll look like a happily domesticated man." The words came out in a bantering manner, but deep inside she experienced a pang of regret that they weren't true. She scowled at herself. Reid Prescott was a close-minded cynic. She was letting the physical pleasure he gave her influence her too much.

Still, a little later, as they walked along the tree-lined streets toward the center of town, his proclaimed attitude nagged at her. Gerald Walker, one of Reid's elderly patients, was out working in his garden. As Reid waved a good-morning to the man, Celina's patience snapped. "If you honestly consider people to be, in general, selfish and self-centered, you can't possibly really care about your patients. So why did you become a doctor? It sure can't be for the money. Doc says you're very talented. He says you'd be a success wherever you chose to practice. You could open an office in a big city and earn a lot of money. Here you'll make a living, but you'll never get rich."

He smiled wryly. "I was told at an impressionable age that I was a natural."

That he had actually admitted to something that had happened when he was young shocked Celina. "Who told you that?" she prodded.

His jaw tensed as if he was going to refuse to answer, then he signed brusquely, "The old doctor who used to take care of my grandmother. Her mind wasn't always clear, so he put me in charge of seeing that she took her various pills in the right sequence. She'd become diabetic, too, but she refused even to try to learn how to use a needle to give herself injections. When I was seven, he taught me. Said I had a knack for it. 'Course my doing it saved him a daily trip to our apartment. Anyway, I discovered that I did like science best in school. By the time I got to high school, I'd become fascinated by the idea of medicine. At first I considered going into research, but then I found I liked the challenge of diagnosing a problem and, hopefully, curing the patient or at least easing their suffering."

His manner, she noted, even when talking about his grandmother was dispassionate. "You consider your patients a sort of analytical exercise," she said, wondering how the citizens of Smytheshire would feel if they ever learned that was how he felt about them.

Reid heard the disapproval in her voice. It grated on his nerves. "I consider each one a personal challenge, and my goal is to make them or keep them as healthy as possible," he signed, his shoulders squared with pride.

His was a practical approach, she had to admit. And he was an excellent doctor. Besides, she'd never believed in judging others. And, she added, it was ridiculous for her to care so much about his attitude. "I suppose that's all anyone can ask of their doctor," she said levelly. Then she extended her hand. "Truce?"

"Truce," he signed back, and accepted her handshake. Still, as they walked along, her disapproval bothered him. From a very early age, he'd stopped caring about other people's approval or disapproval. Why he was giving hers a second thought irritated him.

Celina glanced at him as they turned down Birch Street heading for Main. "If you're going to look so grim, people will think you're already regretting having married me," she said quietly. The thought that this might be the truth stung.

"That would defeat our purposes," he muttered under his breath. He forced a smile. "How's this?" he signed. "Do I look like a man wallowing in wedded bliss, or like some fool who's grinning for no good reason?"

Celina noticed that the smile didn't reach his eyes. She was about to tell him he looked like a man trying to show a brave front in the face of death when suddenly amusement began to gleam in those blue depths.

"Of course only a fool believes in wedded bliss, anyway," he said. "So either way, I should look like the role I'm playing."

"There are a great many who have found wedded bliss and are not fools. My grandparents, for example," she returned, determined not to concede easily to his cynical view of the world.

"And yet you were willing to settle for our arrangement rather than wait for your Mr. Right to come along," he pointed out.

"I figured that since he hasn't come along yet, there *is* no Mr. Right for me," she replied, voicing a suspicion that had been on her mind for a long time. She didn't like admitting it, but she had always felt apart from others, never quite one of the group. She'd attributed this to her deafness. What was curious, she realized all of a sudden, was that she didn't feel "apart" from Reid. They weren't even really friends. Their views of the world were diametrically opposed. And he kept a layer of insulation around himself to make certain no one got too close. Yet, she felt a bond with him. *It's because we're in this together. We're helping each other achieve our goals,* she reasoned.

Reid frowned as he pictured Celina with a faceless Mr. Right. The thought of her with another man bothered him. *I must have more of the caveman's "my woman" mentality than I thought,* he mocked himself.

Determined to turn their conversation to neutral ground, Celina said, "We could use some milk."

Reid nodded. They were approaching Main, a wide street encasing a very prettily kept park with a fountain in its center. On the other side of the street, facing the park, were stores, the bank, the post office and

the police station, which also housed the town offices.

"Dr. Prescott. Celina," a voice called out as the pair
reached the end of Birch and turned onto Main.

Looking across to the park, Reid saw Olivia Stuart.
Seated on the park bench nearby was her husband,
Bruce. Reid gave Celina a small nudge as he waved so
that she would spot the elderly woman, too.

Celina turned to see Olivia gesturing for her and
Reid to come across the street. Olivia and Bruce had
been out of town for the past few weeks. This was the
first time she'd seen them since before she and Reid
had announced their engagement. Time to behave like
newlyweds, she told herself as she forced a wide smile
and headed with Reid toward the older couple to accept their congratulations.

"Our grandson drove us up town this morning,"
Olivia said as Celina and Reid stepped from the street
onto the brick walkway that surrounded the park.
"He's in getting his hair cut. I was going to ask him to
drive us over to your place later. We wanted to offer
our congratulations."

"Thank you," Celina replied.

Noticing that the older woman's attempt at signing
was made nearly impossible by her arthritis, Reid had
begun to sign her words to Celina. When Celina re-
sponded before he'd finished, he realized she'd read
Olivia's lips with ease. Returning his attention to Olivia, he added his own thank-you.

After the amenities had been exchanged, Olivia regarded Reid sheepishly for a moment, then her back
straightened and her gaze shifted to Celina. "I was
wondering if you'd mind touching my hands," she
requested, holding them out toward Celina. "They've

been bothering me mightily. And Bruce's knee kept him up most of the night." Her attention shifted back to Reid. "No offense to you, Dr. Prescott, but our medication doesn't always stop the pain, and we don't want to increase the dosage if we can help it. And neither of us likes those cortisone shots."

Reid's jaw tensed. Then, signing to Celina as he spoke, he said, "If Celina's touch helps ease the pain without the shots, I'm happy for you. But be certain you continue to come see me for your regular check-ups and if you think your arthritis is getting worse."

Olivia frowned impatiently. "Of course we will. That's the agreement we have with Celina." Suddenly she smiled playfully. "'Course I guess you two haven't had a lot of time to talk about us old folks."

"No, we haven't." As he spoke, Reid made a mental note to ask Celina how many others came to see her on a regular basis.

He hid his displeasure well, Celina thought, glancing toward him and seeing only an expression of polite indulgence on his face. But she sensed his anger as surely as she could feel the heat emitting from the pain in Olivia's hands as she took them in hers. She held them, massaging the enlarged knuckles gently until she felt the heat lessening and saw the lines of distress on Olivia's face begin to fade.

"Thank you, child," the woman said, touching Celina gently on the cheek after her hands had been released.

Celina smiled back, then turned toward Bruce.

"Now come sit by me," he said, patting the empty portion of bench beside him. As Celina obeyed and then placed her hands on his right knee, he grinned.

"You're the only woman my wife would ever allow to play with my knee," he said, then laughed heartily.

Celina laughed, also. He'd made this jest a thousand times before, but he enjoyed it and she liked to see him happy. The heat she felt beneath her hands told her that he was in a great deal of pain. Again, she began her gentle massage and slowly the sensation of heat faded.

Outwardly Reid's expression remained unchanged. Inwardly he experienced mixed emotions. He was pleased that the elderly couple seemed to find relief in Celina's touch. But he was irritated by their gullibility in thinking that she was truly responsible. He wanted to tell them that the easing of their discomfort came from within themselves, not from Celina, but he knew they wouldn't believe him.

Main Street had begun to fill with activity by the time Celina and Reid left the Stuarts and crossed over to Langley's grocery. Reid watched as Celina waved to those she saw waving to her. In the store he observed her chatting with several others and the cashier.

As they left Main Street and started back along Birch, he looked over at her. He was carrying a bag of groceries, which prevented him from signing. But in this instance he didn't want to sign; he wanted to find out just how good she was at reading lips. He nudged her shoulder. When she looked up at him, he chose a subject he knew she would never guess he would talk about and said, "There's supposed to be an abundance of shooting stars tonight."

Celina had expected Reid to say something about the Stuarts. Shooting stars didn't strike her as a topic that would interest him. She regarded him skeptically. "Who told you that?"

"Zebulon Lansky," he replied, still wondering if she'd actually understood what he'd said. "While you were talking to Samantha Brant."

Celina frowned thoughtfully. "There's supposed to be magic in a shooting star."

This was the first time Reid had ever heard of anyone claiming there was magic in a shooting star. Recalling what Doc had told him about the founding of Smytheshire, he regarded her narrowly. Maybe Doc didn't know the people of this town as well as he thought he did. She was looking ahead again. He tapped her on the shoulder to get her attention. "Do you believe in magic?"

A rush of unpleasant memories suddenly flooded Celina's mind. "When I was young, my mother used to tell me I could make a wish on the first star I saw each night and that wish would come true. Instead of wishing for different things each time, I decided to wish for what I thought was most important. Every night I wished for happiness. When I was fifteen, both my parents were killed and I became deaf." Her jaw tensed. "No, I don't believe in magic."

Reid felt a rush of sympathy for her while at the same time breathing a mental sigh of relief. Regretting the pain he saw on her face, he tapped her on the shoulder again. "Until today, I never realized how really good you are at reading lips," he said, bringing their conversation back to the reason he'd brought up the subject of the shooting stars in the first place. "I thought, because everyone who knows how to sign, sign to you all the time and translates for those who can't, that you weren't very good at reading lips."

"With people I've known all my life, I can generally understand what they're saying to me," she replied to the question in his eyes. "But most don't really believe that, so they sign and write me notes when they want to be certain I understand what they're telling me. I don't mind. I feel a little more secure that way." She frowned thoughtfully. "With strangers I can't always read their lips, especially if they have an accent. With anyone new, it usually takes me a while to get used to how they form their words." As she said this, she suddenly realized that in Reid's case she'd been able to immediately read his lips almost perfectly. She glanced at him, her gaze focusing on his mouth. Abruptly she found herself remembering how deliciously warm it felt on hers.

You're letting him occupy too much of your thoughts, she scolded herself. She returned her attention to the sidewalk ahead of her. Too tense to remain silent, she rattled on, "Sometimes, it's just a matter of memory. People repeat the same things. For example, that remark Bruce Stuart made about my being the only woman Olivia allows to touch his knee. He says that every time."

Reid again tapped her on the shoulder. "That's something else we need to talk about," he said.

Celina wished she'd bitten her tongue rather than bring up the Stuarts. But she had. Eventually he would have anyway, she knew, adding philosophically they might as well clear the air now.

They had reached their house. He nodded for her to precede him inside. In the kitchen, as she put the milk in the refrigerator, Celina wondered what he would say. If he tried to forbid her from giving comfort where she could, they were going to have a major fight. Steeling herself, she turned to face him.

Although he now knew she had no trouble reading his lips, Reid decided that this was important enough he should also sign. "You realize you're merely a placebo," he said, carefully spelling out "placebo." "The relief from pain that the Suarts believe you give them comes from within them, not from you."

Celina had faced skeptics before. There were even times when she, too, had wondered if maybe it wasn't simply the belief that she could help that eased people's pain. But his know-it-all attitude rankled her. "Well, I suppose it's more flattering to be considered a sugar pill than one that's bitter to swallow," she tossed back.

Reid scowled. He didn't like hurting her feelings, but he had his patients to consider. "I'm not saying there is anything wrong with what you do," he said. "I just want you to understand that you have to send people to me to make certain they get the proper care."

She returned his scowl. "We've already had this discussion, and I've given you my word I would never attempt to practice medicine."

He raked a hand agitatedly through his hair. Normally he didn't care how people felt toward him, but he didn't like her being angry with him. "You're right," he conceded, then heard himself adding, "Debra Ramsey and her baby are doing very well. I appreciate your making her come to see me." He couldn't believe he was actually attempting to appease her. *I just don't want her locking me out of the bedroom,* he told himself. After all, he was only human and he thoroughly enjoyed their physical relationship.

Celina couldn't fault him for having doubts. And being angry with him wasn't going to help her accomplish the goal she sought by this marriage, she reminded herself. "I'm glad she'd doing well," she said levelly, letting him know they again had a truce.

The next afternoon, however, Celina found herself worrying that their truce was going to be short-lived. The morning had passed pleasantly enough. She and Reid had gone to church and then had dinner at the Varley farm with both sets of grandparents and her aunt. Afterward, she and Reid had come home and sat on the front porch reading the newspaper.

Celina had just begun working on the crossword puzzle when Harriet Calfono had come by with Carla, her two-month-old baby daughter, and Samuel, her four-year-old son.

Noticing Reid laying his paper aside, she'd looked in the direction of his gaze to see the woman opening the gate and entering the yard with her children.

"We were just out for a stroll, and I thought I'd come by and visit with Celina," Harriet said, making it clear to Reid this wasn't a professional call, as she continued toward the porch steps.

Smiling indulgently, he returned his attention to his paper.

About halfway to the porch steps, Harriet paused, released the baby carriage and signed a hello to Celina. Then she continued toward the house.

Celina liked Harriet. They'd been classmates and friends throughout their school years. After Celina's accident, Harriet had been one of the first to learn sign language. "I'm glad you stopped by," Celina called out, rising and starting toward the steps to help the woman with her children.

Celina reached the carriage as Harriet lifted the baby out. Taking the child, Celina noted that the little girl's hair was still too sparse to tell what color it would eventually become, but she had her father's brown eyes. The boy, on the other hand, definitely took after his mother, she thought, smiling down at him. He had Harriet's black hair and gray-green eyes, as well as the same-shaped nose and mouth. Harriet took the boy's hand to help him up the steps while Celina led the way toward a couple of empty chairs on the other side of Reid.

Celina seated herself and watched as Harriet said, "Afternoon, Doctor," to Reid. She saw him glance up to give the woman and her son a welcoming smile, then return his attention to his newspaper.

There had been nothing in Reid's manner that should have made the woman feel uneasy, yet Celina was sure she caught an edge of nervousness behind Harriet's friendly smile. *Not only is Reid the new doctor in town, he's also a stranger,* she reasoned, to account for this show of discomfort in his presence. But as Harriet seated herself, Celina noticed that the woman remained stiff instead of relaxing. "Samuel looks as if he's grown another inch just since you all were in the library last week," she said, attempting to put the woman at ease.

The young boy grimaced shyly. His mother had let go of his hand, but rather than moving away from her, he moved closer to her, pressing against her leg.

That behavior wasn't like him, Celina knew. He was usually outgoing. In fact, she'd expected him to go over to Reid and try to make conversation. Then it occurred to her that the boy's shyness was probably due to the fact that Reid was a doctor. Since doctors gave children shots, many children associated them with unpleasant experiences. Satisfied that this was the reason for the boy's hesitation, she turned her attention back to Harriet. "Carla certainly is growing fast," she said.

"Yes." Harriet smiled warmly.

But even the smile evoked by the thought of her baby held a trace of nervousness. "How's Sam?" Celina asked, wondering if the woman was on edge because she'd had an argument with her husband.

"He's fine," Harriet replied, a look of resignation spreading across her face. "He's on his way to California on a long-distance haul. I have to admit, I do hate his being gone so much. But I knew he would be. A woman has to expect that when she marries a truck driver. I knew the kind of life I'd agreed to when I married him and I shouldn't complain. He's a good husband and father." As she finished speaking, Harriet glanced past Celina.

Following the woman's line of vision, Celina saw Reid concentrating on reading the paper, clearly wanting to allow the women to have their chat without his interference. She couldn't help thinking how natural he looked sitting there on her porch. It was as if he belonged there. But he doesn't want to belong here, she reminded herself curtly and she'd be wise to follow Harriet's example and never forget the bargain she'd agreed to. Forcing her mind away from Reid, she turned her attention back to Harriet. The woman appeared decidedly uncomfortable.

"Maybe I should have waited until tomorrow and come by the library," Harriet signed.

It bothered Celina that people would feel ill at ease coming to her home simply because Reid lived there now. "You're always welcome here. Reid and I both enjoy having company," Celina assured her, then glanced toward Reid for confirmation.

Laying aside his newspaper again, Reid smiled. "I would hate to think my presence frightens off Celina's friends."

Harriet's cheeks flushed with embarrassment. "It's not that exactly—your presence, I mean." Her gaze shifted between Reid and Celina. "I feel like I'm imposing. It was silly of me to bother you two on a Sunday afternoon."

"I have never known you to be a silly woman," Celina said, reaching out and touching Harriet's arm as the woman started to rise, obviously planning to leave. "Please, tell me why you came."

Harriet sank back down in her chair. She placed an arm around Samuel's shoulder. "With Sam gone so much of the time and me being so busy with the new baby, I'm afraid Samuel has been feeling a little neglected. Anyway, for the past few days he's been complaining about his stomach hurting. But he hasn't been sick, you know, not throwing up or anything." Her gaze traveled past Celina to Reid. "I know he just wants attention, and to be honest I don't have the money to go running to the doctor at every little complaint." Her jaw tightened defensively. "And I don't want to encourage him to become a hypochondriac like my mother."

Celina had to admit that Paula Bradley was the town's worst hypochondriac. She'd once heard Grandma Tupper suggest that the woman buy a house next to the doctor's office for convenience' sake.

Harriet's gaze had shifted back to Celina. "Anyway, I thought you might take a look at him. Touch his stomach. Just to reassure us he's not really sick,'' she finished self-consciously.

Celina glanced toward Reid. He gave her a dry be-my-guest look. She felt as if she'd been issued a challenge. So much for their truce, she thought as she motioned for Samuel to move near.

''I knew I shouldn't have come,'' Harriet said, watching Reid unhappily, obviously having noticed the exchange between him and Celina.

''I always enjoy seeing you and Carla and Samuel,'' Celina replied, smiling encouragingly as she handed Carla back to her mother and again motioned for Samuel to come to her.

''Go on,'' Harriet coaxed him gently when he remained clinging to her leg.

''Come on, Samuel,'' Celina encouraged.

Hesitantly he approached her, then stood stiffly in front of her.

''Where does it hurt?'' she asked gently.

He pointed to his navel.

Gently Celina ran her hand over his abdomen. On the lower right-hand side she felt the heat. There was something wrong. Continuing to smile so as not to alarm the child, she turned toward Reid. ''Just to be on the safe side, I think a real doctor should take a look,'' she said.

Reid raised a quizzical eyebrow.

''Appendix,'' she signed quickly.

He gave her a skeptical glance, then turned his attention to the boy. ''We men should stick together,'' he said. Then, glancing toward the mother, he added, not quite able to keep the edge out of his voice, ''Besides, if my patients aren't feeling well, I prefer to take a look at them myself.'' Seeing the embarrassment mingled with the distress on Harriet's face, he frowned at himself for letting his temper show. In a less critical, friendlier tone, he said, "I'm sure we can work out a family plan so that you can afford my services."

"I just didn't want to bother you unnecessarily," Harriet replied self-consciously.

"Seeing Samuel is never a bother," he assured her, turning his attention to her son.

The moment he looked away from her, Harriet tapped Celina on the shoulder. "Is there really something wrong with Samuel?" she signed anxiously when Celina turned to her.

"That's up to the doctor to tell us," Celina replied, returning her attention to the boy and Reid. To her surprise, Reid seemed to have developed an instant rapport with Samuel. A look of male camaraderie passed between the boy and the man, and when Reid motioned for Samuel to come to him, the boy obeyed without hesitation.

Reid knelt on the porch as Samuel reached him. "Lie down," he instructed. Gently he prodded the boy's lower abdomen. After a few moments, he turned toward Harriet. "It feels like a possible case of appendicitis to me. I think it would be a good idea to take him into Greenfield to the medical center and run a few tests."

Harriet paled. "He really is sick?"

Celina saw the guilt etched into the woman's face. She turned toward Reid to see him saying, "In many cases with children, until appendicitis becomes acute it is not detected. You were wise to come by here this afternoon. If my diagnosis is correct, we've caught this in plenty of time."

He did have a good bedside manner, Celina had to admit as she glanced at Harriet and saw the guilt on the woman's face subsiding some.

Reid tapped Celina on the shoulder. "I'll drive Harriet into Greenville."

"I'll come, too," she said, feeling that Harriet could use her support. Then turning to her friend, she asked, "Who shall we call to come take care of Carla?"

"I'll call my mother-in-law," Harriet replied, quickly rising from her chair. "My mother can't handle crises."

Celina nodded and led the woman inside to the phone.

During the next few hours, Reid had no time to speak to Celina alone. They got the boy to the hospital, where it was determined that his appendix was indeed swelling and required immediate surgery.

Now the operation was over. It had been a total success and Samuel was in the recovery room.

Harriet's father and father-in-law were with Harriet and Celina in the waiting room. The two men had shown up at the hospital just minutes after Reid, Celina and Harriet had arrived with Samuel. Harriet's mother had remained at home. "She doesn't handle emergencies well," Harriet's father had said to explain his wife's absence. "The news brought on one of her weak spells. I promised to call her and tell her what was happening." Harriet and her father-in-law had nodded knowingly and Reid was sure he'd seen relief on all three faces that Paula had opted to stay home.

Now, as Reid stood by Samuel's bed in the recovery room he smiled down at the boy. "I'm happy to say your grandfather will be able to report to your grandmother that you're doing just fine.''

The boy was still groggy but he was waking from the anesthetic and managed a sleepy smile.

Reid experienced the sense of accomplishment mingled with relief he always felt when a patient was on the road to recovery. "See you tomorrow," he promised. Turning his attention to the nurses, he gave them instructions, then headed to the waiting room. It was time for him and Celina to be going home.

Seeing Harriet suddenly look toward the door, Celina turned that way, also, and saw Reid entering the waiting room.

"I've just seen Samuel," he was saying. "He's doing fine and is being moved to his room." His gaze took in all three members of the boy's family. "The nurse will be in soon to take you to him."

Harriet smiled gratefully. "Thank you, Doctor."

"You should thank Celina, too," Reid replied.

Amazed that he had openly admitted to her aid, Celina was speechless as Harriet thanked her and gave her a hug.

Reid waited until the boy's grandfather had added their thanks, then said, "Celina and I will be leaving now." His gaze focused on Harriet. "But I want you to call me if you have any concerns."

Harriet nodded.

As Celina accompanied Reid into the corridor, she glanced toward him, still stunned that he had admitted in front of others that she'd been a help.

"Only a fool would deny it," he said in answer to the question in her eyes. Then, as if politely letting her know that he didn't want to discuss this further, he said, "I'm exhausted. Let's go home."

He did look exhausted, Celina thought as they drove toward Smytheshire. And, there was no use in trying to converse since the darkness prevented her from reading his lips clearly even if he did look her way. Besides, he needed to concentrate on the road. She couldn't stop wondering, though, if he thought her prediction had been a lucky guess or if he honestly now believed she had a gift. She told herself it shouldn't matter. She'd never cared before what people thought about her ability. She was always just pleased when she could help someone.

But as she and Reid entered the house and he flicked on the lights, she placed a hand on his arm to stop him from going upstairs. "Do you really believe I felt something?" she asked.

Reid studied her solemnly for a moment, then said, "My rational side wants to believe that this incident was a fluke. But Doc's no fool, and according to him, this kind of thing has happened before. I can't ignore Doc's experiences or the business with Debra Ramsey. Obviously you do have a certain diagnostic ability." A tired smile suddenly tilted one corner of his mouth. "You're definitely a very practical wife for a doctor to have."

Celina knew he meant that as a compliment. But she had to force a smile as the word "practical" caused a sour taste in her mouth. Grudgingly she admitted she didn't want him to think of her as a practical wife. *But that's what you are,* she reminded herself, watching him turn away and continue up the stairs to the bedroom. And he was nothing more than a practical husband. What they had was nothing more than a practical marriage. She'd be wise to remember Harriet's words—"I knew what life I'd agreed to and I shouldn't complain." *And I shouldn't complain,* Celina told herself firmly. She should be satisfied if both she and Reid got out of the marriage what they both had bargained for. She was only going to get hurt if she started hoping for more.

In spite of this firm talk with herself, she was still feeling piqued a little later as she joined him in bed. He's a cynic who thinks most people are selfish and self-centered, she reminded herself. But she'd seen the honest concern in his eyes when he'd examined little Samuel. Beneath that cynical shell was a man who cared. Of that she was certain. She was also just as certain that he would never allow anyone to penetrate that shell and touch that caring man. *Stop thinking about him so much,* she ordered herself. But as she lay back and closed her eyes, she felt a tap on her shoulder.

Reid had levered himself up on an elbow so that he was looking down at her. "How does your pain-relieving power work on headaches?" he asked.

She knew it was irrational, but she wished he'd said something tender or caring. "I thought you considered me a source of your headaches, not a cure."

Reid couldn't fault her for this observation. "I know I'm not easy to live with," he admitted. "But I haven't minded being your husband." He'd said this merely to be polite, but as the words echoed in his mind, he realized they were true. *I simply need the physical pleasure a woman can give,* he told himself.

Celina was furious with herself. He wasn't the one making this marriage difficult—she was. She was beginning to want more from him than he'd agreed to give and that wasn't fair. "You're not that bothersome to live with," she said.

Reid experienced a rush of relief. He needed this marriage to achieve his goal, and that was the only reason he was glad she wasn't ready to throw him out, he assured himself. But he did wish his wife didn't look so appetizing. His head began to throb more violently. "Thanks," he said, easing himself back onto his pillow.

The deep lines of pain on his face tore at Celina. She maneuvered herself into a sitting position and began to massage his temples.

"You do have a soothing touch," he said as the hammering in his head faded. His eyes were closed. Lazily he ran his hand along her hip and thigh. Her touch was soothing, but the rest of her was stimulating, he thought.

Celina barely caught his words as the heat of his hand penetrated her light nightgown, awakening desire. Focusing her attention on her hands, she realized his headache was gone. Certain he was too exhausted for any other activity, she said more for herself than for him, "I guess it's time we went to sleep."

Reid knew she had to be tired. *Just one little taste,* he promised himself. "Thank you," he said, opening his eyes and drawing her down onto him for a light kiss.

His hair-roughened chest tantalized her as the warmth of his mouth sought hers. It was dangerous to be so susceptible to him, she warned herself. She had no illusions about this marriage lasting. And she didn't want to be hurt when it ended. But as the heat of his body penetrated hers, the worry about the future was washed away by a flood of pleasurable sensations.

Reid felt her smile against his mouth, and the way she softly brushed against him threatened his control. One hand moved along the line of her body while the other wove into her hair and pulled her head closer, bringing her mouth more firmly against his. When she showed no resistance, his caress became more possessive. He felt her body respond, and thoughts of their tiredness were forgotten.

Later as she lay sleeping beside him, Reid had to admit that he enjoyed being married to her. A satisfied smile played at the corners of his mouth. He'd never believed a woman could spark such fire within him. Helping her conceive a child was a much greater pleasure than he'd expected. Even more comforting, there were no emotional strings attached. They were just two consenting adults helping each other attain their goals.

Chapter Nine

Celina attempted to fight back the wave of nausea, but it was too strong. For the second morning in a row, she ran for the bathroom. A few minutes later she stood staring at her pale image in the mirror. It was barely two and a half months since the wedding. Mentally she ticked off dates in her head. Admittedly she was a couple of days late. But that wasn't unusual.

She frowned nervously. That lucky penny must have been more powerful than she'd thought. She'd hoped to get pregnant quickly, but she hadn't honestly expected it to happen so soon. Of course, she and Reid had been very active amorously. For a moment she even felt a pang of regret that her goal had been so quickly achieved. She'd enjoyed being with him immensely.

Her pregnancy didn't mean that their physical relationship would stop, she reminded herself. But it did mean that as soon as the Smythes gave him the lease for the office he could consider their bargain completed. And he'd probably want a divorce so that he could be on his own again. Well, he was welcome to whatever life he wanted. She would have her child and that was all she wanted.

"Before I start knitting baby clothes, I'd better made certain this isn't just a case of the flu," she murmured. Reid had left the house both mornings before the nausea had struck so strongly she couldn't control it. Last evening he'd been called out on an emergency right after dinner so he hadn't witnessed her sickness then, either. She'd tell him tonight and he could run a test tomorrow to verify her suspicions.

She pressed her hands to her lower abdomen and a sense of joy swept through her. A smile tilted the corners of her mouth. Her nausea was not due to the flu. Even without a test, she was sure of that.

Reid was nearly to Main Street when he turned around and went back home. Celina had looked pale this morning during breakfast. She hadn't looked too well yesterday morning, either. He'd found an excuse to go by the library to check on her yesterday afternoon, and she'd looked fine then. "You're letting her occupy too much of your thoughts," he scolded himself aloud.

Still, he continued back to the house. As he passed through the kitchen and into the hall, he heard her in the downstairs bathroom.

Opening the bathroom door a few minutes later, Celina issued a startled gasp at the sight of Reid leaning against the opposite wall.

"Having a little early morning nausea?" he asked. He'd never believed that at the onset of a pregnancy, a person could tell a woman was pregnant simply by looking at her. But there was no doubt in his mind that Celina was with child.

"It would seem that our amorous activities have been rewarded," she replied. "Of course, you'll want to run a test to be sure."

"Of course." He'd told himself a million times that the baby would be hers. But, suddenly he felt an overwhelming bond with this unborn child. *Not a bond,* he corrected. *What I feel is responsibility.* A coolness descended over his features. "I want you to know that, if you are pregnant, I intend to help financially with the child for its lifetime," he informed her.

So, she had been right, she congratulated herself. He was already looking toward the time when they would be divorced. She felt a jab of hurt. It's just disappointment, she told herself. She enjoyed his company in bed and she'd miss that when he was gone. Nevertheless, the hurt lingered. "That wasn't part of our bargain," she replied stiffly.

The thought of her attempting to shut him out of their child's life annoyed him. "I helped conceive this child. The people in this town will expect me to support it."

Celina studied the taut line of his jaw. It reminded her of a man determined to perform what he felt was his duty. "A child needs to feel wanted, not as if it's merely a financial responsibility."

"True, and I know you will make the child feel wanted. However, raising a child is a big financial undertaking, and I intend to see that ours has whatever advantages I can afford to give it," he stated firmly, signing his words to give them emphasis.

Celina could see that arguing would be useless. Her pride wanted to continue to refuse his aid, but her more practical side knew she would never be able to afford to give their child the advantages Reid could provide. "You may do as you wish."

He nodded. "And now let's run that test to see if this discussion was actually necessary."

A little later, as she opened the library, she noticed that her hand was shaking sightly. The test had been positive. She'd known it would be. She was happy, but she was also nervous. Her baby might not have a traditional set of parents, but it would be well cared for, she assured herself. She could provide the love along with the basic necessities of life. Reid would see that their child received whatever extras he could afford to supply.

But all that was in the future. Right now she had more immediate business to take care of. Her grandparents and her aunt Adelle needed to be told. Reid wanted her to start on prenatal vitamins right away. He'd been going to write a prescription, but she'd asked him to wait a day. She'd been born and raised in this town. She knew that the moment she walked into Faraday's Drugstore with her prescription, the news of her pregnancy would spread like wildfire and she wanted to be the one to tell her grandparents and her aunt.

As soon as Brenda came in to work, Celina left her in charge of the library and walked over to her aunt's dress shop.

"To what do I owe this unexpected visit?" Adelle asked as Celina entered.

Celina glanced around to make certain they were alone. When she turned back toward Adelle, her aunt was studying her narrowly. "You're pregnant," Adelle signed with assurance.

Celina stared at her. "How did you guess?"

Adelle pursed her lips. "A big clue was the way you looked around to make certain no one was here—as if you had a secret to impart you didn't want overheard." She grinned. "And then there's that nervous little way you have of screwing up your mouth when you've got something to tell me and you're not sure how I'll react."

Celina had to admit she was worried that her aunt might think the pregnancy had occurred too soon. "Well, how are you going to react?" she asked.

Adelle laughed. "With a hug," she said. She reached Celina in two long strides and gave her a tight squeeze. Then, stepping back, a serious expression came over her face as she again studied her niece closely. "I know this is what you wanted. But how is Reid taking it?"

"He's pleased," Celina replied honestly. "He knew I wanted a child."

Adelle's smile returned. "Then all's well in paradise." Again her gaze narrowed. "Have you told your grandparents?"

Celina shook her head. "I just found out myself this morning."

"This is a woman's moment," Adelle signed with authority. "I'll call your grandmothers and invite them here for lunch today. You can show up as a surprise and tell them."

Celina gave her aunt a hug. "I knew you'd help."

* * *

To Celina's relief lunch went very well. Both grandmothers were excited and happy for her. And if they thought she'd behaved imprudently by getting pregnant so soon, neither said so. Admittedly she'd seen some anxiousness in their faces until she'd assured them that Reid was also pleased. Then they'd relaxed and spent the rest of the meal talking about babies.

As she walked back to the library, Celina breathed a sigh of relief.

"Dr. Prescott came by while you were gone," Brenda informed Celina when she returned. "I told him you were at Adelle's, and he said to say he'd see you at home this evening." Brenda suddenly looked worried. "You two haven't had a fight, have you?"

"No," Celina assured her.

Brenda looked embarrassed. "I didn't mean to pry. It's just that he looked sort of gruff or concerned or something like that. I guess maybe he'd had a difficult patient and was still a little on edge."

"Probably," Celina replied noncommittally, wondering if Reid was having second thoughts about fatherhood and regretting having entered into this bargain.

Brenda grimaced. "Some of the people in this town can be real pains." Abruptly she glanced toward the door.

Celina followed her gaze to see the Mellon sisters entering. "I'll take care of them while you eat your lunch," Celina said, glad of the excuse to escape Brenda's theorizing about the reasons for Reid's mood.

For the next hour she tried to put Brenda's description of Reid out of her mind. But it continued to nag at her. If he had decided he wasn't pleased with the thought of parenthood, then that was his tough luck, she told herself. He'd agreed to their bargain. Still, she grew more tense. Finally she left Brenda in charge of the library again and walked over to Reid's office.

"He's just finishing with a patient," Glenda informed her. "You can wait in his office, and I'll tell him you're here." Celina noticed that Glenda's usual smile was missing. "Has it been a difficult day?" she asked, hoping Glenda would say they'd had a particularly difficult patient.

Pushing her chair back to give herself plenty of room, Glenda began to sign. "Let me put it this way." An impatient frown replaced her mask of calm control. "If you and Dr. Prescott had a fight this morning, I hope you're here to patch things up because he's been a bear to work for today."

Celina's stomach threatened to knot. "I'll do what I can." But as she turned away and walked toward Reid's office, she didn't know what she could do. She certainly wasn't going to give up her baby.

Entering the office, she went to a chair by the desk and sat down to wait. Then anger took control. In the next instant she was on her feet, leaning against his desk, glaring at the door. He had no right to be irate about her pregnancy! She saw the knob turn and her back stiffened defiantly.

Reid frowned worriedly when he saw her face. "What's wrong?" he asked gruffly, taking another step into the office and closing the door behind him to ensure their privacy. "Was your aunt upset to learn about your pregnancy?"

She scowled at the expression of concern on his face. "My aunt and both my grandmothers were very pleased."

"Then why are you looking so grim?" he asked, signing his words to give them emphasis.

She regarded him impatiently. "Because I told them you were pleased by the pregnancy. Obviously you aren't."

"What makes you think that?" His expression was that of someone unjustly accused.

Her scowl deepened. "You've got Brenda and Glenda thinking we've had a quarrel, and who knows how many others. Clearly, after you had time to think about our situation, you decided you were sorry you'd gotten yourself involved."

Reid drew a harsh breath. "Maybe I shouldn't have," he admitted. "I've told myself it would be easy to think of this child we were creating as *your* child." He slammed his fist into his hand to emphasize the *your*. "But I feel a responsibility to it and to you."

"I didn't ask you to," she snapped back. "This is *my* child." To give this declaration strength, she, too, slammed her fist into her hand.

Reid rubbed his face agitatedly. "I know. But I've been worried about you and *your* child all day. It occurred to me you probably haven't kept anything substantial down for nearly two days now. That's why I went by the library. I wanted to see if you'd been able to keep your lunch down."

He looked like a man caught between a rock and a hard place. She'd never meant for him to feel trapped in this sort of dilemma. "Yes, I kept my lunch down. My aunt and grandmothers were full of advice and remedies for my nausea. Besides, most women go through this, and both they and their babies turn out fine."

"I know, I know." He grimaced. "But being a doctor, I know all the complications that can arise."

Fear for her child filled her. "Is there any reason to suspect I might have some of those complications?"

He shook his head. "No. You're a perfectly healthy woman under the age of thirty."

Celina breathed a sigh of relief. Then her scowl returned. "I am also going to be one of the unhappiest soon. When your staff and Brenda hear about my pregnancy, they're going to assume you're not pleased, and that should spread around town faster than a prairie fire."

"Then I'd better practice some fire prevention before I have two angry grandfathers demanding to know why I'm not pleased," he said. "You wait here."

His admission that getting involved with her had been a mistake hurt. *I'll make certain he understands he isn't responsible for either me or my child,* she promised herself.

She'd been glaring at the door once again. Abruptly it was opened. She relaxed her face into a less hostile expression as Glenda, Karen and Doc entered, followed by Reid. While the other three formed a line in front of her, Reid took a position by her side.

"I want to apologize for my behavior today," she saw him say. "I know I've been a little sharp, but I've been nervous and feeling a little intimidated." He paused and smiled that sheepish smile of his, the one that always caused her heart to beat a little faster.

Glancing at the others, Celina saw tiny smiles at the corners of the two nurses' mouths and knew they weren't immune to this small show of charm, either.

Doc, she noticed, was watching with an expression of calm indulgence, but she saw the worry in his eyes.

Reid placed his arm around Celina's shoulders and grinned broadly. "We just discovered this morning that we're going to be parents," he announced.

He looked the part of the nervous but proud father-to-be, Celina thought as she watched him. She knew it was just an act, but she was grateful.

"That explains why you've been on edge," Glenda said with a nod. Signing toward Celina, she added, "It's a known fact that doctors make the worst patients. But it's also been my experience that they make even worse expectant fathers. They worry about every little thing."

"That's for sure," Karen added. Then both women crossed to Celina and gave her hugs of congratulation.

After congratulating Reid, also, the nurses left to go back to work. Doc stayed behind. He waited until the door was closed, then studied Reid and Celina closely. "I hope this marriage is working out well," he said. "I'd hate to think I talked the two of you into something you're regretting."

"You offered us a solution and we took it," Reid replied. "We're adults. There's no reason for you to feel responsible for what happens. Celina has what she wanted, and if I get my lease, then we've achieved our goals and there will be joy all around."

Doc frowned. "I was hoping your arrangement would work itself into a real marriage," he said with an expression of regret. "I guess I'm no good at matchmaking."

"You did just fine," Celina assured him. "I have no regrets." But Reid's admission that he did still nagged at her. Her jaw firmed as she again promised herself to find a way to convince him that he owed nothing to her or the child.

Doc's gaze shifted to Reid. "This pregnancy should give Brian the final incentive he needs to agree to give you the lease."

"Then we'll all have what we want," Reid said. He knew Doc was asking for more assurance from him that he was pleased with how this arrangement had worked out, but he couldn't give it. He'd never expected to feel such a strong sense of responsibility toward Celina or their child. *Guess I'm not as detached from the human race as I've tried to be,* he mused. Feeling the need to escape, he glanced at his watch. "I've got a patient waiting. See you two later," he said, and left.

As the door closed behind Reid, Doc turned toward Celina. "He's treating you well, isn't he?"

"He's treated me very well."

Doc looked relieved, then disappointed. "I guess I'm turning into a silly romantic in my old age, but I was hoping you could break through that hard shell he keeps around himself. He hides it well, but I've seen real caring in his eyes when we're discussing our patients."

"Life has taught me to take the bitter with the sweet," she said gently. "You offered me an opportunity to have what I wanted in a way that would be acceptable to my family. For that I will always be grateful. And I hope Reid gets his lease so that he will have what he wants."

Doc gave her a hug. Then stepping back, he signed, "You know where I am if you need anyone to talk to about things you don't want to discuss with your aunt or grandmothers."

"Thank you," she said. After giving him another hug, she left.

As she passed through the waiting room, the grins she received from Glenda and Karen let her know they'd fully bought Reid's explanation of his behavior. And back at the library, as she informed Brenda of her pregnancy, she put on a convincing act of being the indulgent wife of an overly protective husband.

Overly protective was an understatement, Celina thought as she stared at Reid across the dinner table that night. He'd just informed her that he'd decided to hire Emily Sayer to come in once a week and do the housecleaning.

"And I'm hiring Josh to do the yard work," he finished firmly.

"I thought exercise is supposed to be good for a pregnant woman," she protested.

"You have a full-time job. I don't want you overworking yourself and getting run-down," he replied. "And since you've already told your family about the pregnancy, I stopped by Faraday's Drugstore on the way home and picked up your vitamins."

Celina had to admit that if he wanted this baby as much as she did, she would have enjoyed this show of solicitude. But she knew the real reason behind his actions. "You don't have to try to buy off your responsibility, Reid, because you have none. I wanted this baby and you helped me. You've done your part. You don't owe me or the baby anything further."

Reid's expression grew grim. "I thought I made it clear earlier today, that I'm not the kind of man who can sire a child and then walk away and never look back. I thought I could, but I can't. You're going to accept my help whether you like it or not."

Celina's anger flared as he once again made it clear he felt trapped. But just as she was about to scream at him that she didn't want anything from him, her fair side stopped her. It wasn't right to be angry with him for not wanting to feel bound to her and the child. After all, he hadn't planned on that complication and it obviously distressed him. "I suppose I should be grateful to have someone to help with the housework," she said, instead.

He nodded his agreement and began eating.

That he was so distraught by his sense of responsibility continued to grate on her nerves. Unable to stop herself, she said tersely, "It's perfectly natural for a parent to feel a kinship to their child. In fact, it's normal."

Cynicism etched itself into his features. "For some it might be natural, but it's not that way with all parents," he replied sharply. Then with a look that said this discussion was at an end, he returned his attention to his food.

Celina wanted to reach across the table and touch him, hoping she could bring him some comfort, but she held back. Reid Prescott, she now knew, was a man with wounds that ran deep, wounds that would probably never heal.

"Apparently your pregnancy was the final push Brian Smythe needed," Reid announced when he returned home from the office a couple of days later.

"He came in today and offered me the lease. I told him I wanted security and asked for a ten-year contract. He gave me fifteen. We sign the papers next week. I take over the practice in January. Doc's going to stay on a part-time basis. He says total retirement would give him too much time on his hands."

"I'm happy for you," Celina said, and she was. But even as she spoke, she felt a wave of apprehension. She hadn't expected Brian Smythe to act so quickly. Forcing herself to speak the words aloud, she said, "I guess once the papers are signed, our bargain will be completed."

Reid nodded. He'd expected to experience a sense of freedom. Instead he felt something akin to regret. "Figured for appearance' sake, I'd stick around until after the baby is born and for a while after that." This, he'd decided, was reasonable. But he'd never forced his company on anyone and he wasn't going to start now. "Of course, if you're tired of having me around, you can kick me out anytime."

Celina wished she knew if he really wanted to stay. Her pride refused to keep him there if he wanted to be free. "I don't mind having you around," she replied honestly. "And you're right. For appearance' sake, it would be easier if you stayed at least until the baby is born. But I don't want you to feel you have to remain if you want to go."

A part of him did want to leave. He couldn't deny that. But he heard himself saying, "If I leave too quickly, Brian might try to renege on the contract. And I wouldn't want your grandfathers organizing a mob to tar and feather me for leaving you alone and pregnant. Guess it would be best all around if I stay."

It bothered Celina that his only reason for staying was to avoid trouble. But then their whole arrangement had been based on acting in a practical manner, she reminded herself. "You're probably right. You wouldn't look too good in tar and feathers."

Reid experienced a sense of relief. Earlier today, after Brian had offered him the contract, he'd told himself he wouldn't care whether she wanted him to stay or not. Now, he assured himself, he still didn't care. The relief he was feeling was because remaining here would make his life go more smoothly. He also admitted that she looked darn cute in those shorts. And even cuter out of them, he added. He told himself he should practice some restraint. On the other hand, he argued, he might as well enjoy her company while it lasted.

"I was thinking of taking you out to dinner to celebrate," he said, moving toward her.

"I'm not too sure I should eat in public just yet," she replied.

"I was going to help you dress," he coaxed, reaching for her and beginning to unbutton her blouse.

She wished she had more resistance, but as his fingers brushed her skin, the fires of passion ignited. "Seems more like undressing than dressing," she observed.

It suddenly occurred to him she might not feel like participating in the activity he had in mind. "Maybe I should just take a cold shower," he said, backing away.

Here's my chance not to just melt in his arms, she told herself. This was immediately followed by the thought that when he was gone, she'd regret having passed up this opportunity. "Why don't we move this conversation upstairs and I'll help you undress while you decide what you want to do,'' she suggested.

In the next instant she was being scooped up into his arms and carried up the stairs. *As long as I take each day as it comes and keep in mind that he won't stay forever, I'll be fine,* she assured herself.

Chapter Ten

It was two weeks before Christmas. "Time to buy a tree," Celina announced during dinner.

Reid, she admitted, had endured the huge family Thanksgiving gatherings surprisingly well. So that all the out-of-town relatives who hadn't been able to make it to the wedding could get to know him, the two of them had had to attend both the Warleys' and the Tuppers' Thanksgiving celebrations. On Friday they'd gone back to the Warleys for leftovers, and on Saturday back to the Tuppers for a final feast. By Sunday, Reid had sworn if he ate another bite of turkey he'd begin to grow feathers.

But he'd survived the four-day holiday weekend admirably and impressed her relatives favorably. To her grandparents and his aunt he'd not only been polite, he'd even shown warmth. To the rest of the family, he'd been friendly. He'd laughed at cousin Fred's terrible puns and hadn't displayed the least bit of impatience when Aunt Sophie kept forgetting the punch lines to every joke she tried to tell. But Celina knew him well, and she'd noticed that his laughter never reached his eyes. Instead, she'd sensed a cool detachment beneath his facade of amicability as if he was mentally keeping everyone at an arm's length.

Afterwards her grandmothers and her aunt had mentioned noticing his stiffness every once in a while, but they attributed it to his being overwhelmed by so many new relatives.

During the past weeks while they shopped for Christmas presents and she'd begun decorating the house, he'd entered these activities with the same kind of attitude he used when they went grocery shopping on Saturday mornings. To him, these were simply a part of the season's routine that had to be taken care of.

But when she mentioned getting a Christmas tree, Celina could have sworn she saw a flash of emotion in his eyes. Then it was gone, and she thought maybe she'd simply imagined it. Lately, it seemed as if she'd been telling herself almost hourly that she wasn't interested in learning about the real Reid Prescott, the man he kept locked up inside, but each day this felt more and more like a lie. Just once, she wished he would let down his guard. But he wasn't going to and she was a fool if she thought she could change him, she admonished herself.

Still, she couldn't stop herself from studying him covertly as they tramped through the rows of trees. It seemed to her that he was uneasy, but then, he might just be trying to maintain his patience, she conceded.

It was cold and damp and she was insisting on looking through the entire maze of trees before choosing one.

"Are you sure you don't want to take a second look around?" he asked dryly when she finally made her selection, thus confirming her suspicion that his patience was near an end.

"No, this one will do," she replied.

"Good, because I was beginning to worry I might turn into an icicle before you'd made up your mind."

Again she chided herself for thinking that this expedition might have touched the man inside. Clearly he was simply anxious to get in out of the cold.

It was nearly nine by the time they got the tree home and set up in a stand.

"It's beautiful," she said, stepping back to admire the nearly six-foot evergreen that now occupied the space in front of the living-room window. "We'll put the lights on it tonight. They're the hardest. Then we can do the rest of the decorating tomorrow evening."

"You're the boss," Reid said. "I haven't decorated a tree in years. You'll have to give me instructions."

Again Celina thought she saw an uneasiness in his eyes, then it was gone, replaced by an expression of patient indulgence.

By the time they had untangled the lights, checked for burned-out bulbs and hung the five strings of miniature lights on the tree, she was exhausted. Reid, she noted, looked as tired as she did.

"The rest of the decorating is definitely going to have to wait until tomorrow," he said, unplugging the lights.

Watching him, for a moment Celina could have sworn he looked as if he wanted to run from the room. In the next instant, the cool, detached expression on his face caused her to chide herself for imagining something so silly. They were both just tired, she told herself and followed him up the stairs. As if to prove her point, Reid fell nearly instantly asleep. Again admonishing herself for letting him occupy too much of her thoughts, Celina also drifted into slumber.

Reid awoke in a cold sweat. He'd been dreaming. It was an old nightmare. One he hadn't had in years. One he thought he'd successfully willed himself never to have again. He glanced at Celina, hoping he hadn't woken her. To his relief, she was still sleeping peacefully. For a long moment, he lay motionless. He told himself to go back to sleep. But instead, memories tormented him. Carefully easing himself out of bed, he went in search of some aspirin.

Celina began to awake as the bed shifted gently. She felt a sudden chill. Still half-asleep, she reached for Reid. The warmth of his body lingered where he usually lay but he wasn't there. She opened her eyes and looked around the dark room. He wasn't there, either. A sense of aloneness so strong it felt like a physical force came over her. Staring into the shadows, she lay there waiting for him to return.

But he didn't come back.

"He must have had an emergency call," she murmured, sitting up and switching on the bedside lamp. But there was no note on the pad lying there. She frowned. He always left a note when he had to go out.

She looked at his pillow. "He's a big boy. He can take care of himself," she told herself. "Go back to sleep." But even as she gave herself this order, she tossed off the covers.

"He was probably having trouble sleeping and is down in the den reading one of his medical journals," she muttered, furious with herself for caring so much about his whereabouts. Still, she found herself pulling on her robe and heading for the door.

As she reached the bottom of the stairs, a twinkling of tiny lights caught her attention. Turning toward the living room, she saw that the Christmas tree had been lit and Reid was standing in front of it. He was barefoot and dressed only in his old flannel robe. His hands were shoved into the pockets, and his shoulders were squared as he stared at the tree. He reminded her of a man set for battle. She approached him and touched him lightly on the arm. He jerked around, and she realized he had been so engrossed in his thoughts he hadn't heard her. "Are you all right?" she asked.

No was the answer that flashed into his mind. Abruptly he pushed it aside. He'd faced down these old ghosts before. He'd face them down again. "I'm fine," he signed.

The moonlight coming in through the window, plus the multicolored lights of the tree illuminated his face, and Celina saw the haunted look in his eyes. "You don't look fine," she stated bluntly. The sudden fear that he would resent her interference filled her, but an even stronger need to offer him solace would not allow her to turn away.

"Buying the Christmas tree and decorating it brought back some old memories," he admitted. Suddenly images from the past flooded his mind. They were so vivid it was as if he had been transported back in time. "My grandmother and I always bought and trimmed a tree. I was five when my mother left me with her. She'd been forty when my mother was born and was nearly sixty-eight when she inherited me. She was widowed, living off social security and a pension my grandfather left. My parents both sent money on a fairly regular basis. It wasn't much, but it was enough to supplement what she had so that we always had food on the table and a roof over our heads."

Celina's gaze flickered from his hands to his mouth as he spoke and signed. There was a distant expression on his face, and she had the feeling that the signing was being done automatically and he'd forgotten she was there.

Reid had made it a practice never to talk about his early years. They were past. Nothing could change them. He'd survived them, and he thought he'd pushed the most hurtful and anger-producing of his memories so far into the hidden recesses of his mind that they would never emerge again. But the nightmare had returned, and with it those memories he most wanted to forget. Even worse, they were as strong and as vivid as if they'd happened yesterday. He ordered himself to shut up, but the words continued to flow. "The roof over our heads was a one-bedroom apartment in Queens, New York. I slept on the couch." A smile played at the corners of his mouth. "I didn't mind the arrangement. I had free access to the kitchen and could watch television all night. Grandma Krenshaw was practically deaf, so she never heard me.''

Celina watched the smile disappear. Anger suddenly flashed in his eyes. ''I can still remember my mother telling me that I had to behave. She swore she wanted me with her but she couldn't manage taking care of me while she traveled around the country looking for a job.'' He gave a shrug as if to indicate that this didn't really matter. The anger faded.

''My grandmother was sickly and had advanced arthritis. I was already fairly adept at taking care of myself. I knew how to get cereal out of a box and pour milk into it and how to make peanut-butter-and-jelly sandwiches.'' He smiled wryly. ''I remember that because my mother kept assuring my grandmother that I could fix my own meals if necessary.'' Again he shrugged as if to say this didn't matter any longer, and his expression became distant. ''Anyway, my grandmother and I worked out a comfortable living arrangement. She took care of me and I took care of her.''

Celina recalled his once telling her he'd been in charge of seeing that his grandmother took her medicines. He'd even given her insulin shots. She realized he'd never had a real childhood. At the age of five, he'd had to take on the major responsibility of taking care of himself.

Reid fell silent as the images from his nightmare descended upon him. A cold sweat beaded on his brow.

Celina saw his pain. She also sensed a terror. ''The two of you must have made a very good pair,'' she said, attempting to ease his mood.

"We did," he conceded. His jaw tensed. "Then she died." A shiver shook him. He was living the nightmare again. He was ten years old. He'd just come home from school and entered the apartment. His grandmother was sitting in her favorite chair. "I found her. Her eyes were open. The television was on. She seemed to be watching it, but I knew something was wrong. I tried to talk to her. When she didn't respond, I panicked. I shook her and begged her to answer me." His mouth twisted into a grimace. "Actually, according to the neighbors, I was screaming at her at the top of my lungs. Guess you could say I was trying to wake the dead. But it didn't work." His expression again became distant. "The neighbors came and called the doctor. The O'Malleys from across the hall took me in for the night."

He drew a harsh breath as his grandmother's image began to fade. "I remember wondering if they'd let me stay with them or if I could get a job and keep my grandmother's apartment. Late that night I heard Mrs. O'Malley on the phone. In the five years I'd known her, I'd never heard her utter a swear word, but I heard her that night. I knew she'd been trying to call my mother. Around two in the morning the phone rang. 'I don't give a damn about your passionate nature and your feeling the need to have a few days to get over the shock of this news,' I heard her saying. 'You get yourself here tomorrow. You've got a boy to collect and a mother to bury.'" Reid stiffened at the memory of his mother having to be ordered to come get him.

Celina saw hurt mingled with anger in his eyes. When her parents had died, she'd been surrounded by people who loved her and wanted her with them. But it hadn't been that way for Reid. She pictured him as a young boy, unwanted and alone. She searched for something to say, but all that came out was, "That must have been a difficult time for you." *Of course it was, stupid,* she answered herself.

Reid tensed. He didn't need or want her sympathy. He was furious with himself for having told her so much. These were his private demons.

Celina saw the expression of cold detachment she'd grown so used to spread across his face.

"It taught me to rely only on myself," he replied. He recalled being fifteen and asking Jo if he could stay with her. That was the one time he'd forgotten the lesson he'd learned when his grandmother died. He wouldn't forget it again. Putting an end to this conversation, he signed forcefully, "It's cold down here and it's late. We should be in bed getting some sleep." Turning away from her, he unplugged the lights of the tree.

A few minutes later, Celina was back in bed. Reid was there, too. But he was on his side and she was on hers. She knew that was the way he wanted it.

When you agreed to this marriage, you knew he was determined never to allow himself to become emotionally involved with you or anyone, she reminded herself. Now she knew how deeply he was committed to that resolution. And she was only going to get hurt if she allowed herself to become emotionally involved with him. Still, she could not force herself to turn away from him. He'd been hurt deeply, and in spite of his obvious wish to shut her out, she wanted to comfort him. "My feet got cold and now I'm chilled," she said, turning toward him. "I can't seem to get warm."

Reid looked at her. He didn't like seeking solace from anyone other than himself. But just the thought of holding her seemed to ease the harsh memories that continued to plague him. He lifted his arm and offered her his shoulder.

She slid over to him and snuggled against him. She wished she could heal the wounds of his childhood, but was more convinced than ever that they were too deep.

Wrapping his arms around her, he lay holding her. A soothing heat like that of a soft summer sun spread through him. Any woman's gentle touch would have relaxed him, he told himself as he drifted into a peaceful slumber, his nightmares again pushed into the dark recesses of his mind.

The next morning Celina noted that Reid was more distant than ever. But then, she'd expected that. For the next few hours, she kept reminding herself of Jo's mother's advice. She also recalled that her grandmothers had said the same thing, only more bluntly. "You'd better be able to live with a man's faults, because he's not going to get rid of them," both of them had told her many times. Even Harriet Calfono's words played through her mind. "I knew the kind of life I'd agreed to and I shouldn't complain," she'd said.

But as she sat eating lunch, Celina again found herself wishing she could break down the barriers Reid kept around himself. She breathed a disgruntled sigh.

Even if she did break down his barriers that didn't mean he would fall in love with her.

Love. The word caused the food she was swallowing to catch in her throat. That was the root of her problem. She'd been telling herself that this increasing closeness she felt toward him was simply a hormonal thing caused by the fact that he was the father of her child. Now she was forced to admit that was a lie. She'd seen beyond the cynical shield he worked so hard to keep around himself and she'd fallen in love with him. *Idiot!* she screamed mentally. *Just don't let yourself start hoping he'll ever feel the same or you're going to get hurt.*

Chapter Eleven

It was February. Celina had respected Reid's unspoken wish not to talk about his past again. They'd settled into what, on the surface, was a comfortable routine of coexistence. But beneath the surface, his ability to remain detached was wearing on her nerves. Some days she found herself thinking that life might be easier if she simply did ask him to leave. At least that way she wouldn't have to worry about how she would face that event when it did take place. But then she'd think about his being gone, and a loneliness that not even her baby could fill would come over her. Maybe he would decide to stay and maybe he would even learn to care for her, she'd finish.

"And as long as I don't let myself start believing that really could happen, I'll be fine," she muttered to herself as she held this debate again. This time it had been triggered by the flowers and box of candy he'd brought her the day before. Yesterday had been Valentine Day. When he'd walked in that evening with gifts, she'd been stunned. She'd fixed his favorite meal and dessert, but she hadn't expected anything from him. She hadn't even been going to mention that it was Valentine Day.

When he'd said she deserved the roses and candy for putting up with him, happiness had brought a flush to her cheeks and her hopes had blossomed. Then he'd mentioned that Adelle, Glenda, Karen and Doc had all reminded him of what day it was. "If I hadn't gotten you something, my name would have been mud," he'd added. Her flush of pleasure had faded.

"The man is driving me crazy," she growled, frowning at the clock on the bedside table. It was ten o'clock at night. Debra Ramsey had gone into labor early that afternoon. Reid had asked Glenda to come by the library to tell Celina he wouldn't be home for dinner and wasn't certain how late he'd be. At nine, she'd felt exhausted and gone to bed. But she hadn't been able to fall asleep.

A fluttering movement deep within jerked her mind away from Reid and back to the main reason for her sleeplessness. The flutter, she knew without a doubt, was her child moving. She laid her hand on her slowly enlarging abdomen. The thought of the new life within both thrilled and frightened her. She'd felt the first small flutter a couple of weeks earlier and the uncertainty she'd been fighting ever since suddenly overwhelmed her.

Her eyes brimmed with tears. She hated crying. She almost never gave in to it. But lately, even the smallest of problems seemed to bring the threat of tears.

Her grandmothers and Aunt Adelle had assured her this was normal. Nevertheless, she scowled irritably at herself and blinked the tears away. As her lids flickered, she was suddenly aware of the blurred image of someone standing over her. Her vision cleared and she saw Reid. He looked tired, and he was watching her with an expression of concern.

"Are you ready to talk to me about whatever has been bothering you the past few days?" he asked.

He was the last person she wanted to talk to. She gave a shrug as if what she had on her mind was inconsequential. "I'm just having those moods pregnant women have because of overactive hormones or whatever."

He regarded her with a patronizing frown. "When you wept over that ridiculous commercial two nights ago, that was hormones. And the temper tantrum you threw when you burned the cake the other day, that was hormones. But this anxiety I've seen on your face lately is more than some simple hormonal upheaval."

Embarrassment reddened her cheeks. "It's really nothing important," she assured him. Yawning widely, she rolled over and closed her eyes.

She had an effective way of closing a discussion, Reid fumed. All she had to do was turn her back or close her eyes and he was completely blocked out. The thought that maybe he didn't really want to know what was bothering her occurred to him. But he'd never been the kind of person to avoid the truth. His hands closed around her arms and he turned her onto her back.

Celina was tempted to squish her eyes shut and refuse to converse with him. But that would be extraordinarily childish. Besides, he'd be there in the morning. Giving in to the inevitable, she opened her eyes.

Reid faced her levelly. "Is it me? Am I getting on your nerves?"

"No," she replied. Then it occurred to her he had his lease and maybe was looking for a comfortable way out of their arrangement. Pride caused her to add, "But if you're getting bored with this marriage, you're free to go."

Her offer of freedom irritated Reid. She was pregnant with his child. It was his duty to see her through this. "I wasn't offering to leave," he said, signing the words sharply. "I'm staying until I'm satisfied that you and the baby are going to be all right."

Celina wanted to shout at him that she didn't want him to stay because he felt an obligation to her and the child, but she bit back the words. She didn't want to fight with him. Hot tears of frustration, caused by the fact that he hadn't learned to love her, were already forming at the back of her eyes. Not only could a confrontation at this moment make her end up crying in front of him, she might also reveal how she felt. That would embarrass her and put an unfair strain on him. "Now that that's settled, the baby and I need our rest," she said, again turning on her side and closing her eyes.

Reid glared down at her. He was always cautioning husbands that pregnant wives had to be treated with kid gloves, that their bodies were going through changes that could bring on mood swings and cause even the mildest-tempered woman to become difficult to live with. Now he could speak with real authority, he thought. Again his hands closed around her arms and again he turned her onto her back. When she opened her eyes, he released her and signed forcefully, "Nothing has been settled! I want to know what is bothering you."

Celina's jaw hardened. She knew what he'd say if she told him what was nagging at her, and she didn't want to hear it. "It's nothing important," she replied firmly.

Reid scowled at her. "You're not a frivolous woman. That much I have learned living with you. And even if what is bothering you is frivolous, it's still affecting your peace of mind." The look of command on his face grew stronger. "If you won't talk to me, then go see Adelle or your grandmothers. It's not healthy for you or the baby to keep worries and concerns locked up inside."

Celina's chin trembled. "I can't talk to them, either."

Reid studied her narrowly. He'd hoped that whatever was bothering her was actually something minor that her pregnant state had blown out of proportion. But that she was refusing to talk to either her aunt or her grandmothers increased his worry. "Then you're going to have to talk to me," he signed in sharp movements that offered no compromise.

The baby fluttered again. Celina knew she had to talk to someone, and although Reid would not have been her choice, there was no one else she was willing to tell. Shifting into a sitting position, she met his gaze. "You'll just get that cynical look in your eyes and tell me it's a little late for second thoughts," she said.

A coldness spread through Reid. It would seem she was going to add more validation to his view of the world. "And are you having second thoughts?"

She saw the self-righteous icy glimmer in his eyes. "Not second thoughts exactly," she replied defensively. Her jaw firmed as she laid her hands protectively on her abdomen. "I want this baby. I'm just not sure I'll be a good mother."

Reid read the fierce love on her face and knew that his child would fare much better than he had. "You'll make an excellent mother," he said, signing his words with firm conviction.

Surprised by his unqualified support she studied him guardedly. "You aren't just saying that to make me feel better, are you?"

"I may not always tell you what you want to hear," he replied, "but I will always tell you the truth."

His assurance gave her confidence. The doubts she'd been having faded, and she was able to relax again. "Thank you," she said.

"You're welcome." Yawning he added, "I'm exhausted. I'm going to take a shower and then come to bed."

Watching him walk away, the wish that he thought she made as excellent a wife as she would a mother flashed through her mind. You can't have everything, she chided herself.

The problem is, she thought one pleasant spring afternoon in June, she couldn't stop wishing for more. The day was so pretty she had walked to work this morning. Now she was on her way home. She glanced down at her rounded abdomen and smiled. Her pregnancy was what her grandmothers referred to as being in full bloom.

She couldn't say that Reid hadn't been attentive. In fact, in many ways he'd been overly so. The nursery was a good example. Once she'd chosen which room she was going to convert into the baby's domain, he'd pointed out that she shouldn't be lifting heavy furniture. Then, allowing her only to give directions, he'd proceeded to clear the room out himself including everything from the furniture to the lamps and pictures. Once the room was emptied, he'd said the paint fumes were dangerous for the unborn child and insisted on painting the walls and ceiling alone while she went to visit her aunt. She knew he was right on this point and hadn't objected. But when he'd insisted on cleaning and waxing the floor by himself, as well, she thought he was going too far. Then he'd brought her old crib down from the attic and refinished it by himself, again only allowing her to give instructions. And he'd insisted on paying for any new furniture she felt she needed to purchase.

He'd also been overly indulgent with gifts. Lately, almost weekly, he'd bought something either for her or the baby or both. A month ago he'd come home with the latest TDD because it had an answering machine built in. "This way, if you're busy with the baby, you won't have to stop what you're doing to answer the phone," he'd said. Yesterday, he'd presented her with a signaling device. The thing operated sort of like a paging machine. One part, which reminded her of an intercom, was to be placed in the room where the baby was. A small boxlike piece resembling the beepers doctors used was to be carried on her person. When the baby cried, that piece would vibrate to let her know she was needed.

She breathed a frustrated sigh. Although she knew he was simply trying his best to be thoughtful and helpful, the gifts grated on her nerves. "The only thing I want from him is his love," she murmured under her breath. But Reid was determined not to fall in love, and if there was one thing she'd learned about the man it was that when he'd made up his mind, he stuck to his resolve.

As Celina drew closer to home, the sight of a battered green pickup truck parked in front of her house caused her to tense. Thoughts of Reid were vanquished. That truck belonged to Rycroft Gerard. Of course, no one ever called him Rycroft. He preferred Ryder and people respected this preference. They respected him. Celina also knew most people were at least a little intimidated by him. She didn't like admitting it, but she was one of them. He was a big man, standing six-two, muscular from a life of hard work on his farm. He was also a quiet man who kept his own counsel. She also knew him to be a good, decent person. In fact, she liked him.

What had caused her to tense was the fact that this was Thursday. Emily Sayer came to clean on Thursdays and she would still be there. Everyone in town knew that the Gerards and the Sayers were not on speaking terms. Celina had actually seen members of one family cross the street so they wouldn't have to walk past a member of the other family. But right now Ryder and Emily were in her home. Together. Alone.

Picking up her pace, she reached the house just as Reid pulled into the driveway. She saw Ryder ease his long frame out of one of the rocking chairs on the porch. As Celina went through the gate, Emily came out of the house. She was carrying her purse and obviously leaving. There was a cool, controlled expression on the woman's face. Passing Ryder without even a glance, she descended the stairs and reached Celina about halfway down the walk.

Celina smiled encouragingly as Emily began to sign with the slow deliberation of someone new to this method of communication. Emily also spoke her words and there was apology on her face. "Josh couldn't come to mow the lawn today. He had a lot of homework to do," she said. Resolve replaced the apology. "But he'll be here tomorrow for certain and he'll weed for free."

"Tomorrow will be fine," Celina assured her. "And I insist on paying him for any work he does." Before her last word was out, she saw Emily's expression turn to fury and the woman twisted around. Ryder had joined them. Obviously, he'd said something that had upset Emily. Celina noticed that Reid had also joined them. She quickly flashed him a message asking him to tell her what Emily and Ryder had said to one another.

Reid signed back that Ryder had said he was sure he'd seen Josh down by the river this afternoon. Emily had told him that her son's activities were none of his business.

Celina caught a glimpse of the final hostile look Emily shot at Ryder before she turned back to Celina and Reid. Her expression once again apologetic, Emily began to sign and speak. "The truth is my son is going through a difficult time. He had a crush on Amy

Buckley that didn't work out too well, and he's been a little moody lately. But he'll be here tomorrow. I promise."

"I understand," Celina assured her.

"Thank you," Emily said gratefully. Then without a backward glance at the man who had caused her discomfort, she continued toward the street.

Celina's attention shifted to Ryder. He was watching Emily's departing back with a cool, calculating look in his eyes. She liked both Ryder and Emily. But she would never invite both of them to the same party. She saw Ryder's attention shift to Reid and realized that Reid had spoken to him.

"I brought a gift for the baby," she saw Ryder say to Reid. He motioned toward the porch. "Tell Celina it's a thank-you for easing some of my mother's pain, especially during those last months when her cancer was so advanced."

Celina glanced at her husband. She'd expected to see at least a hint of disapproval in his eyes, but his expression remained politely neutral as he signed Ryder's words to her, obviously wanting to make certain she'd understood everything the man had said.

"I was glad I could help," Celina replied.

Ryder smiled and his rugged features softened. "You'll make a good mother," he said assuredly.

"Thank you." When he wasn't looking so grim, he could actually be considered handsome, she thought.

Tipping his Stetson hat, he added a quick goodbye and left.

Going up onto the porch, Celina and Reid discovered a wooden baby cradle. It was hand-tooled and stained a deep cherry color. "Ryder has a reputation for fine woodworking," Celina said, leaning down and touching the highly polished surface. "It's his hobby. This is beautiful." She glanced at Reid to see if he agreed.

"It's very nice," he confirmed. Reaching down, he caught her by the arm and helped ease her into a straightened position. His expression was solemn. "Apparently Emily is having some trouble with Josh."

"I'm sure she'll be able to work it out," Celina replied. "She and her son are close. They've been through a lot together."

Reid regarded her narrowly. "I just want you to know that I'll always be available if you ever need help with our child." Without waiting for a response, he picked up the cradle and carried it into the house.

Celina's chin threatened to tremble. He was letting her know he would come if she needed him but would not be staying with her. Her shoulders squared; that had always been their agreement. The baby kicked as if in protest. Soothingly she patted her abdomen. *We'll do fine on our own,* she assured her unborn child.

The urge to go inside and tell Reid he could pack and leave that night was strong. But she knew he'd refuse. He considered it his responsibility to remain until after the baby was born and she had her strength back. Besides, she was in no mood to face her family and explain why her marriage was breaking up before the child was even born. And if she hadn't gone and let herself fall in love with the man and start hoping for things that could never happen, she wouldn't have been caught in this dilemma, she admonished herself. She should be pleased that Reid was as good a man as he was and that he was being so supportive of her and the child, and forget about wanting anything further from him. With these thoughts firmly in mind, she went inside.

Chapter Twelve

Celina sat in a rocking chair on her front porch. It was a hot Wednesday in July, a week and a half past her due date. She'd been dressing for work when she'd felt the strong contraction. There had been other milder ones that morning but she'd had contractions before and knew that a couple of mild ones didn't mean she was going into labor. She hadn't even mentioned them to Reid. But as the strong one reached its peak, she knew her child would be born this day.

Reid had already left by the time this occurred. He'd wanted to make an early-morning house call on the Stuarts before going to the office. She'd kept track of the time between the strong contraction and the next. It had been a full twenty minutes. They were too far apart to call Reid home just yet, she'd decided. She'd called Brenda and told her that she wouldn't be in to work. Then she'd put on a comfortable, light-weight cotton maternity smock, gathered her knitting and gone out to the porch.

As she sat rocking, enjoying the warm, sweet morning air, she heard Doreen Troy running the vacuum sweeper inside. "Strange things do happen in this town," she murmured to herself. Emily Sayer had gotten married and had given up her housekeeping jobs to run her own household. And since Doc didn't really need Doreen on a daily basis, she'd taken over Emily's once-a-week cleaning chore at the Prescotts'.

Celina's face screwed up into a thoughtful grimace as she thought about Emily's marriage. She and probably most of the other residents of Smytheshire were still in a state of shock about that union. Emily Sayer had married Ryder Gerard. Actually, Emily's marriage had given Celina some hope for her own. But that hope had faded swiftly. Strange things can happen, Celina admitted in frustration, but Reid Prescott falling in love with her didn't appear to be one of them.

Another strong contraction pushed her frustration to the back of her mind. She glanced at her watch. The last two contractions had been ten minutes apart. A tap on her shoulder made her look up, and she saw Doreen standing beside her chair.

"Seems to me it's about time to call Reid," the woman said, signing her words with authoritative movements as she spoke.

When Doreen had arrived this morning, she'd immediately guessed why Celina wasn't dressed for work. And for the past three hours, she'd been hovering over Celina like a mother hen. Better her than Reid, Celina had told herself. However, Doreen was right. The time had come to call her husband.

Reid sat behind the wheel of his car trying to concentrate on the road as he drove Celina to the medical center in Greenfield. Doc would be handling the delivery of the baby. Reid had called him and he was on his way.

Reid had planned on having Doc or Doreen drive Celina to Greenfield when her time came. He would cancel his later appointments but attend to the patients who were already waiting in his office. Instead, when Celina called, he'd told her he'd come home immediately and take her to Greenfield himself. He'd been in the middle of a routine exam on John Colby. He'd stopped, told the man to make an appointment to come back in a couple of days, gone into his outer office, determined that there were no emergencies, then apologized to those who were there and left.

The palms of his hands were damp. He'd been sure he'd be able to handle the birth of Celina's child with the same professional calm he handled all births. But even in life-threatening cases, he'd never been this nervous.

He glanced at her. Her hands were pressed against her abdomen. He tapped her on the shoulder to get her attention. "Is everything all right?" he asked when she looked his way.

"Everything is fine," she replied, smiling gently. Then the smile disappeared and she grimaced as another contraction began.

Forced to stop at an intersection, he again looked at her. As the contraction eased, he tapped her on the shoulder once more. "Can you really tell if there are complications when it's your own body you're touching?" he asked, signing the words to be certain she understood.

"I think so," she replied.

Abruptly Reid jerked his attention back to his driving. He'd sounded as if he actually considered her diagnosis on the same level as that of a medical instrument. Well, he couldn't deny she did have a knack for spotting trouble. He groaned as he realized he was beginning to truly accept her ability. *I'm letting this birth affect me too much,* he chastised himself.

As if to give further proof of this, he heard her panting, and experienced something very much akin to panic. It was only natural, he decided in the next instant, for him to be more concerned than usual. After all, he was partially responsible.

Celina studied the hard line of Reid's jaw. She had expected him to treat the birth of her child with the same calm, authoritative command he used when dealing with his other patients. Instead, he was behaving like an expectant father. A very tense, not too pleased, expectant father, she qualified. "Maybe you should have let Doc drive me to the hospital," she blurted, hating feeling like a nuisance.

It occurred to Reid that having Doc handle this delivery entirely on his own might have been the smart thing to do. But deep inside, a part of him wanted to be present at the birth. He pulled over to the side of the road. Scowling at her, he curtly signed his words as he spoke. "I told you I would be here for you and I meant it." Then without waiting for a response, he pulled back onto the road.

Celina had seen the fierce protectiveness in his eyes. It would have thrilled her had she not known he was only there because of his strong sense of duty. At least, I know my child will have the best medical care available, she told herself philosophically.

A couple of hours later as Reid sat in the labor room trying to concentrate on a magazine, he wondered again if maybe he wouldn't be wiser to let Doc handle this delivery without him. Doc was sitting calmly drinking a cup of coffee and watching television. But Reid couldn't relax. He sensed Celina's pain almost as if it were his own. And even though his medical training told him that both she and the baby were doing well, he couldn't shake the sense of apprehension that hung over him.

The complications that could arise played through his mind. The thought of anything bad happening to Celina caused a cold chill. His jaw tensed as he promised himself that he'd make certain she came to no harm. He'd never made that promise before. His practical side knew it was foolish. There were always things that could happen over which he might have no control. The thought that he would willingly give his life for hers flashed into his mind.

Scowling at himself for allowing her to affect him so strongly, he returned his attention to the page in front of him. But his mind refused to focus on the words. Giving up on the attempt to read, he set the magazine aside and rose. Noting that Celina was panting, he quickly moved to the bed. Whatever happened to the cool detachment he'd trained himself to feel? he asked himself, as he found himself wishing he could suffer some of the pain for her.

Celina had her eyes shut as she concentrated on her breathing and tried to relax during the contraction. At the zenith of her pain, she felt a hand gently pressing against her abdomen. A warmth spread through her. Without opening her eyes, she knew the hand belonged to Reid. As the contraction lightened, she stopped panting and looked up at him. The warmth his touch had caused turned to a chill. "I wish you wouldn't look so guilty," she growled. "What I'm going through is perfectly natural. It was my choice."

Looking down at her, Reid wanted guilt to be the reason he was feeling the way he was. And, it is, he assured himself. Aloud, he admitted, "I hate seeing you suffer."

Celina's gaze shifted to her abdomen. "It's worth it," she said with certainty.

A few hours later, Reid wondered if she still thought the baby Doc had just delivered was worth the pain she'd suffered. His last glimpse of her face before he'd turned his attention to assisting Doc in bringing the infant into the world had sent a wave of anguish through him. She'd looked exhausted, her face pale and beaded with perspiration.

"It's a boy," Doc announced, with a wide, pleased grin.

Reid looked down at the baby boy Doc had placed in his hands. Then he held the child high where Celina could see him. "You have a son," he said.

"A son," she repeated with a tired but happy smile.

He saw the joy in her face and his question was answered. It was obvious she thought this baby was worth all she'd gone through.

"Welcome to the world. Welcome to Smytheshire, little man," Doc said. Turning his attention to Reid, he added, "You can have the honor of cutting the cord."

Lying the newborn on Celina's stomach, Reid cut the cord while Doc watched.

"And now I'll attend to the mother," Doc said, giving Celina a warm smile and wink before he again sat down at the end of the table.

"You're a lucky boy," Reid murmured to the child, as he handed him to one of the attending nurses who took the baby to clean and weigh him.

"Seven pounds, two ounces," the nurse announced to the assembly as another nurse recorded the information for the birth certificate. Then turning to grin at Reid, she said, "Congratulations, Doctor. How does it feel to be a father?"

"Scary," Reid replied honestly. A sudden sense of pride filled him as the nurse placed the clean, bundled baby in his arms. *This is my son. No, not "my" son,* he corrected. *This child is Celina's son. But if the baby or she ever needs anything, I'll do my best to see they get it,* he vowed.

Celina smiled at the baby as Reid placed him in her arms. Then her attention shifted back to Reid. He looked beat. He was smiling at the nurses. She caught enough of what they were saying to know they were teasing him about being a new father. But she knew that smile. It was a mask. It didn't reach his eyes. He's probably glad this part is over and wishes the next months were too, she thought.

Her gaze shifted back to the baby. A warmth filled her. At this moment, she didn't care if Reid Prescott would be glad to be rid of her. She had a beautiful, healthy baby boy and that was all that mattered.

Reid paced the living-room floor. The time had come, he told himself. This was the hardest thing he'd ever done in his life. But putting it off wasn't going to make it any easier.

Upstairs, Celina stood looking down at her sleeping baby. He was three months old today. He had Reid's blue eyes. She'd named him Kenneth after her father. Just looking at him caused a soft glow of joy.

"But the poets and philosophers are always saying that with every joy there comes some pain," she murmured quietly. "I was hoping they were wrong, but in this case, I guess they're right."

Reid's image filled her mind. She couldn't deny the uneasiness she'd sensed in him since the baby's birth. He'd tried to hide it. But he'd been too protective, too solicitous and too helpful ever since she'd come home from the hospital. The only thing he hadn't been too enthusiastic about was resuming their physical relationship. He had made no advances toward her at all. This, she had to admit, was causing her a great deal of frustration. And some anger, she confessed. She breathed a regretful sigh. "I had hoped he would learn to care for us enough that he'd want to stay," she said, gently stroking Kenneth's cheek. "But I'm afraid that all he feels is trapped. Apparently my lucky penny's power has all been spent. I have no regrets, though. I have you. And now the time has come for me to set Reid free." Leaving the baby's room, she went in search of him.

Reid turned to face her as she entered the living room.

"I guess the time has come for you to leave," she said, reciting the line she'd been practicing all day. It had taken until midafternoon before she'd been able to make herself say the words aloud. But now they were out. She'd kept her end of the bargain.

He'd been thrown out before, Reid reminded himself. But it had never felt this painful. The speech he'd been practicing vanished. "Do you want me out tonight or is tomorrow soon enough?" he signed.

Celina swallowed the lump that had formed in her throat. She'd expected him to leave, but she hadn't expected his departure to be so abrupt. It was as if he couldn't get out fast enough to suit himself. Well, if that was what he wanted, then she would be happy to see him go. "Tomorrow is fine. But you're free to go this minute if you prefer," she said evenly.

Reid nodded. "I'll sleep in the guest room tonight. Tomorrow I'll move back in with Doc."

That he didn't even want to spend another night in her bed hurt. The urge to grab his things and throw them out onto the front lawn was strong. But she'd end this with dignity. "Fine," she said, then she turned away from him and she went back upstairs.

She wanted to scream or throw something. Instead, she went in to see her child. "The bitter with the sweet," she murmured. Well, she'd certainly gotten both this time.

Leaving the baby's room, she went to the hall closet and pulled out fresh sheets. Then she went into the guest room and began making the bed.

Downstairs, Reid stood in the center of the living room. He hadn't moved from that spot since Celina had left him. Suddenly he started walking toward the stairs. When he reached them, he took them two at time. He found her in the guest room.

Celina straightened from tucking the sheet in. A prickling on the back of her neck caused her to turn toward the door. Reid was standing there.

Reid had told himself he'd come up here to tell her that he intended to continue to see his son because that was what the child was—his son, as well as hers. But when she turned to face him, the words stuck in his throat.

"I'll have your room ready in a minute," Celina said stiffly. She was tempted to tell him he could finish making his own bed. But she didn't want him to guess how much she was hurting. *Just be calm, cool and collected,* she ordered herself. Still, afraid the pain she was feeling might show on her face, she quickly returned her attention to the bed.

Tell her you intend to continue to see your son, Reid again ordered himself. He considered approaching her and tapping her on her shoulder to regain her attention. But just the thought of touching her threatened his control. Instead, he stood watching her.

Walk past him as if you don't care, Celina commanded herself as she finished with the bed and turned back toward him. But her legs refused to move. He was still in the doorway blocking her exit. The thought that he didn't even want to be in the same room with her caused a sharp jab of pain. Her shoulders squared with pride. "I'm leaving. You can come in now," she said dryly.

Reid tensed. *Tell her you want to visit your son,* he ordered himself again. But when he opened his mouth to speak, the request he'd been wanting to make for weeks came out. "I want to stay," he said.

Celina stood frozen, afraid to believe what she thought she saw him say. Then her mind swung to Kenneth. That was why he wanted to stay. She had nothing to do with his request. "You don't have to stay with me just to see your son," she said.

Pride caused Reid to want to let her believe that Kenneth was the only reason he'd made this request. But he couldn't. Celina was worth the risk. Reid's jaw set in a grim line as he began to sign and speak. "I love our son, but he's not the reason I'm asking you to allow me to remain here. I know I'm not what you consider good husband material. But I love you. I want to stay with you."

These words had not come easy. Not only had he promised himself he would never ask anyone to let him stay in their life, he'd assured himself he was too smart to allow an emotion, especially love, to influence his actions. But in nearly the same breath he'd asked her twice if he could stay and proclaimed his love for her as well.

Watching him standing there with his feet slightly apart and his shoulders squared, it occurred to Celina that he looked like a man braced for a blow. He'd shoved his hands into his pockets as if to signal that he'd said what he had to say and now the decision as to what to do about it was up to her. He'd said he loved her, and she wanted to believe him more than she'd ever wanted to believe anything in her life. But she'd never been one to turn away from the truth. "You haven't been the most attentive husband since I returned from the hospital," she said. "In fact, you haven't touched me."

A self-conscious expression came over Reid's features. "I was afraid that if I made love to you again, I wouldn't be able to make myself leave you. And I had agreed that our marriage would end if that was what you wanted."

Celina stood indecisively. She wanted to believe it was her and not their son who was making him say these things, but she was still afraid.

Embarrassment spread through Reid as he watched her standing there, saying nothing. He felt like a fool. Obviously she didn't feel the same about him and was looking for a way out. "I'm sorry. I've made you uncomfortable. I'll pack and get out of here tonight."

The thought of his going was more than Celina could bear. "No!" She raced toward him as he turned to leave. Catching him by the arm, she jerked him to a halt. "I've spent so much time trying to convince myself that you could never fall in love with me that I just need some reassurance."

His gaze burned into her. "I love you, Celina," he growled, signing the words with sharp movements to give them emphasis. "I'll do whatever you want to prove that to you."

She saw an anguish that matched her own reflected in his eyes. "You just have," she said shakily. Reaching up, she stoked his jaw. "I love you, Dr. Prescott. I want you with me always."

Reid drew a breath of relief as he put his arms around her in a possessive embrace. Just standing there holding her brought intense pleasure. He'd missed the feel of her so much he'd ached inside.

The heat of his body permeated her senses, sending currents of joy through her. "Kenneth is asleep," she said, kissing his jaw. "And you and I have some making up to do."

Reid wanted to shout from the sheer exhilaration he felt just knowing she truly wanted him in her life. Instead, he simply smiled down at her. "I do love your touch," he said. Then he kissed her with the promise of a very energetic night ahead.

Later, tired but relaxed from their lovemaking, Cellna smiled softly as she lay snuggled against Reid. She was certain no woman could feel more prosperous than she did. After all, love was much more valuable than mere gold.

Tomorrow she would go in search of a locket large enough to house her penny, she promised herself. That coin deserved a special place, a very special place.

Levering himself up on an elbow, Reid studied her with a lazy grin. "A penny for your thoughts."

She grinned back at him. "It's funny you should say that. I was just thinking about a penny."

He frowned in confusion. "You were thinking about a penny?"

"A very special penny," she replied. "I'm thinking about finding a locket I can keep it in."

He cocked an eyebrow quizzically. "This must be a very, very special penny."

She traced the line of his jaw with her fingertip. "You're the one who's very, very special," she said softly.

The blue of his eyes deepened. "You and me together is what is special. Thank you for inviting me into your life and allowing me stay."

A sense of total completeness enveloped Celina. "You're very welcome," she assured him, drawing him back down toward her as the fires of passion once again kindled within her.

*   *   *   *   *

SMYTHESHIRE, MASSACHUSETTS.

Small town. Big secrets.

**Silhouette Romance invites you to visit Elizabeth August's
intriguing small town, a place with an unusual legacy
rooted deep in the past....**

THE VIRGIN WIFE (#921) February 1993
HAUNTED HUSBAND (#922) March 1993
LUCKY PENNY (#945) June 1993
A WEDDING FOR EMILY (#953) August 1993

Elizabeth August's SMYTHESHIRE, MASSACHUSETTS—
This sleepy little town has plenty to keep you up at night.
Only from Silhouette Romance!

MEN MADE IN AMERICA

Fifty red-blooded, white-hot, true-blue hunks from every State in the Union!

Beginning in May, look for MEN MADE IN AMERICA! Written by some of our most popular authors, these stories feature fifty of the strongest, sexiest men, each from a different state in the union!

Two titles available every other month at your favorite retail outlet.

In July, look for:

CALL IT DESTINY by Jayne Ann Krentz (Arizona)
ANOTHER KIND OF LOVE by Mary Lynn Baxter (Arkansas)

In September, look for:

DECEPTIONS by Annette Broadrick (California)
STORMWALKER by Dallas Schulze (Colorado)

You won't be able to resist MEN MADE IN AMERICA!

INTIMATE MOMENTS®
10TH
Anniversary

Celebrate our anniversary with a fabulous collection of firsts....

The first Intimate Moments titles written by three of your favorite authors:

NIGHT MOVES	Heather Graham Pozzessere
LADY OF THE NIGHT	Emilie Richards
A STRANGER'S SMILE	Kathleen Korbel

Silhouette Intimate Moments is proud to present a FREE hardbound collection of our authors' firsts—titles that you will treasure in the years to come, from some of the line's founding writers.

This collection will not be sold in retail stores and is available only through this exclusive offer. Look for details in Silhouette Intimate Moments titles available in retail stores in May, June and July.

Is your father a Fabulous Father?

Then enter him in Silhouette Romance's

"FATHER OF THE YEAR" Contest
and you can both win some great prizes! Look for contest details
in the FABULOUS FATHER titles available in June, July
and August...

ONE MAN'S VOW by Diana Whitney
Available in June

ACCIDENTAL DAD by Anne Peters
Available in July

INSTANT FATHER by Lucy Gordon
Available in August

Only from

Silhouette
R O M A N C E™